THE *Secret* OF A TELLTALE DIET

ANURADHA RAMACHANDRAN

Readomania

Readomania
An imprint of Kurious Kind Media Private Limited
readomania.com
email: contact@readomania.com
Facebook: facebook.com/iamreadomania
Twitter: twitter.com/iamreadomania
Instagram: iamreadomania

First Published in 2022 by Readomania

ISBN: 978-93-91800-18-5

Typeset in Palatino Linotype by Shine Graphics
Printed in Delhi

Author's Note

The aim of this book is not to get everybody on a diet! It is to urge you to do whatever brings you joy, boosts your confidence and propels you to spread your wings and fly.

While the 20s are a joyride (albeit fraught with obstacles), the 30s are when you reconsider and re-work your priorities. The 40s are a totally different ball game! You are more mature and confident because you've figured out some stuff about life and yourself. You realise that your past mistakes don't define you, so if you want to change gears/give up your job to follow your passion/walk away from a caustic relationship/re-look at exercise/diet as a means to stay fit and healthy, then please do it!

Having said that, while dieting/exercising/staying thin may seem like a first-world problem; it requires a lot of courage, discipline, and perseverance. I have seen many fall along the way. Some hide behind the cloak of "stop body shaming" or "I'm comfortable in my skin" because they're just plain lazy! I know this sounds harsh but it is true. You need fire and passion to achieve anything in life and weight loss is no different. So, keep the fire burning and happy reading!

Anuradha Ramachandran

1

March 2012, Solitaire, Hiranandani Gardens, Mumbai

6 am

A robotic digital sound pierced the stillness of the morning. Siya pushed the covers aside, reaching out to stop the alarm and slowly sat up. Turning around to check if Samar was still sleeping, she switched off the AC. He was curled up without a quilt. He liked the bedroom to be cold while she preferred it to be comfortably cool. Leaning over, she covered him up and made her way first to the children's bathroom to switch on their geyser so they could have plenty of hot water to bathe without fighting over who had consumed how much! Siya's day had begun.

For the next ten minutes, she was in auto-pilot mode—kettle on for hot water to make her tea, coffee machine on for decoction (Samar preferred to drink coffee) and milk in the boiler; grating ginger to add to her tea, opening the fridge to take out eggs, bread, and Nutella. After the ginger had boiled furiously for a few minutes in the pan, she added the tea granules and let it boil again. A minute later, after a ladle full of milk had been added and the flavours mingled well, she strained the tea into two cups. Her full-time help, Vaishali, walked into the kitchen with a smile on her face. Handing over the second cup, she informed her what to make for the kids' breakfast and tiffin and also what to prep for Samar's breakfast and lunch. Then, Siya took her cup of tea, two Marie biscuits and headed out to the balcony to enjoy the sounds of silence.

Half an hour later, it was time to wake the kids up. Aryan was seven and always late, and Arjun, still a baby at four. Siya started by drawing the curtains aside and called out to them gently, one by one. They stirred in their beds and rolled over. Opening their cupboards, she pulled out their uniforms and hung them on the door. She called out to them again before heading to the bathroom to fill a bucket with hot water. When she came out, they were still lying with their eyes shut.

Siya was beginning to feel the known stirrings of irritation. "Aryan, wake up now. It's seven already, I've been trying to wake you for the last ten minutes. You have to bathe in time so Arjun can also finish his bath. Hurry."

"Wake him up first then, *na*. Let me sleep some more," he replied, keeping his eyes shut tight. Muttering under her breath, she pulled aside his quilt with a whoosh and whacked him softly on his thigh. "Owww, why are you hitting me?" he cried out.

"I'm not hitting, just trying to wake you up" she retorted. Hearing the commotion, Arjun opened his eyes and started crying. "What are you crying for?" Siya asked in exasperation.

"You're hitting Bhaiya," he declared between sobs.

"I'm not hitting him. I'm just trying to wake him so both of you can be ready on time," she yelled.

Samar walked in just then, rubbing his eyes. "What are you all doing? Arjun, stop crying. Aryan, wake up now. Siya, calm down. This is becoming a circus every morning," thundered Samar, before leaving the room. Reluctantly, Aryan got out of bed and walked zombie like into the bathroom. Siya picked up Arjun and carried him to the bathroom counter. As Aryan got into the shower cubicle for a bath, Siya started brushing Arjun's teeth. All the time, shouting instructions to both the boys.

Half an hour later, they were ready and seated at the table for breakfast. As Aryan tucked into his eggs quietly, Arjun looked sullen. "What happened? Why are you not eating, Arjun?" Siya asked.

"The smell is making me puky," he said, in a small voice.

Siya rolled her eyes. "Why? It's made the same way you like it!"

"It's smelly," he repeated.

"No, it's not. Look, Aryan is eating the same thing. Now, please don't fuss and waste time."

"Siya, don't force him. What do you want to eat, Arjun?" Samar asked as he turned the pages of the newspaper he was reading.

"Porridge!" Arjun answered with glee.

"Vaishali, make some porridge for Arjun," Samar instructed.

Siya turned to look at him, her eyes flashing with anger. *If I'd done this, he would have said you are pandering to them and letting them dictate to you. When I was small, I ate whatever my mom put in front of me, even if I didn't like it. I was never even asked what I like. You give them too many options!* Siya sat quietly, not saying a thing, because she didn't want to fight.

Ten minutes later, Vaishali brought Arjun's porridge to him in a bowl. "Why does he get what he wants while I have to eat egg every day?" Aryan demanded.

Siya looked at Samar. "It's okay, *beta*. He's not liking the smell today. He will also have an egg tomorrow. Right, Arjun?" Arjun shook his head to indicate a no.

"Not fair," Aryan quipped, pushing away his half-eaten breakfast. Just then, Arjun spooned the porridge into his mouth and yelled in pain.

"What happened?" Siya rushed up to him with concern. His face turned red as he started crying. Siya looked under the table—*did Aryan kick him by any chance? You never know with these boys*, she fumed. "Tell me, what happened?" she finally yelled when he wouldn't stop crying.

"It's so hot!" he answered when he finally found his voice.

"Of course, it's hot. Didi just made it," she yelled, losing her patience.

"How would he know, Siya? He's a child. Vaishali should have cooled it before bringing it," Samar admonished her.

Grabbing the bowl from the table, Siya took it to the kitchen and added some cold milk. Stirring it constantly, she sat next to Arjun feeding him a spoonful, taking care to blow on it. A glance at Aryan's face told Siya that he was now unhappy. The clock on the wall chimed just then. Gosh. It was 8 am. They should be leaving the house now. Aryan got up to fetch his school bag from his room. "Didi, have you seen my pencil box?" he yelled, as he rummaged through his bag. Vaishali, who was around to help out, went into his room to look.

As they frantically looked for the pencil case, Siya began to fret. "This is precisely why I tell you to ready your school bags at night. You are going to be so late for school."

"I'm going to be late because of Arjun and his porridge," Aryan snapped back. Before she realised what she was doing, she whacked him hard on his bum.

The ten-minute walk to school seemed never ending as they trudged on in absolute silence. Fear kept the boys quiet while Siya was dealing with her guilt.

At the school gate, as she bent down to kiss them, she found herself holding back tears. They waved to her forlornly and walked away; their sad faces imprinted on her heavy heart. Not wanting to bump into any of the other moms, Siya turned around and walked away briskly, her mind in utter turmoil.

I'm such a horrible mother! Always screaming and losing my patience...but what to do? They don't listen. How many times do I need to wake them up? It's so irritating. Why can't they just be up on time? And then the fussing over food...uff! They are the ones who will be late eventually and get scolded by their teacher. Why don't they understand?

When she walked back into her house, she was relieved to see that Vaishali had prepared Samar's lunch. She was laying breakfast on the table when Samar walked in, ready for work, in his formal attire. "Did they get to school okay?" he asked her. Pulling out a chair beside him, Siya nodded mutely. She was feeling wretched after whacking Aryan but didn't know what to do about it. "Why the long face?" Samar gently asked, oblivious to the tumult within her.

"It's nothing," she said, eating her breakfast quietly. As they had breakfast together, bringing each other up-to-date on mundane matters, Samar's phone alarm buzzed. "Oh, today is the annual day party in our building, Siya. I had put a reminder so we don't miss it."

"Oh God, Samar, do we have to go?" Siya was in no mood to socialise.

"It'll be good to meet other residents. We only know our neighbours on the floor," Samar reasoned.

"Who have not been friendly despite my attempts."

"Precisely why we must meet others, Siya. I'm sure they are all not the same." Samar retorted.

The conversation was over. Samar stood up to collect his laptop and lunch bags, gave her a peck and headed out.

Siya sighed. *I must figure out what to wear for it then.*

2

A heap of party clothes lay scattered over the bed. Siya was standing in front of the mirror, trying to zip herself into a beautifully sequined, off-white Zara top that she had bought only six months back. She sucked in her tummy, held her breath and tried to stretch her right arm above her right shoulder to reach the zip. No matter how hard she tried and how much she held her tummy in, her hand just wouldn't reach the zip to be able to pull it up. *Damn, when did my boobs grow so big?* she wondered, eyeing her reflection critically. *I have to figure out what to wear to the dinner soon. First impressions make a big difference. I'd like them to see me as a modern homemaker; not some frumpy housewife who wears a nighty at home all day long. At this rate, I won't get anywhere.*

Giving up on that top, she rummaged through the hangers in her cupboard for something else to wear. She spotted a black and white printed dress, made of a soft, viscose type material. *Hmmm…dresses are what everyone is wearing these days. This looks like it should fit.* She tried to slide the dress over her head. It slid down to her shoulders and stopped. *Damn*! She tried to pull it down gently but it wouldn't budge. The dress just wouldn't come down her chest. Siya was afraid she would either rip her dress or dislocate her boobs permanently if she yanked too hard!

Bloody hell! What am I going to do now? These stupid clothes used to fit me till a couple of months back. Could it be that they have shrunk? You wish, Siya… If I'd tried them on earlier then I could have gone to the mall and got myself something new. I don't have time now. Tears stung her eyes as a wave of frustration washed over her. *Now, I won't be able to get anything else done. I'll get depressed at how fat I have become, I'll wallow in pity, I'll seek comfort in food, and I'll become fatter.* Giving up on any more dress trials in frustration, she yanked the door of her bedroom open with more force than was required and headed straight to the kitchen.

Born with a sweet tooth, Siya ensured that her kitchen was always stocked with chocolates, cookies, ice cream, Indian sweets, Nutella...you get the drift. Picking up the box of Lindor Truffles, she opened one ruby wrapped truffle and popped it in, savouring the gooey chocolatey treat... *Yummm, there's nothing like chocolate.*

Vaishali walked in. "What happened, Didi?" she asked, perplexed at seeing Siya standing with her eyes closed.

"Oh, nothing, Vaishali."

"Didi...you are always lecturing your kids on how bad this is for their teeth," she said, as she carried on.

Siya froze. *Did she just reprimand me? How dare she? I understand that she means well, having been with us for a while but this is too much. First, the clothes don't fit and then the help behaves like she's my mother!*

"I'm not a child, Vaishali. I know what's good and bad for me," she said, in measured tones, trying to keep her cool.

Sensing that she had antagonised Siya, Vaishali offered to make her some tea. "Sure. Don't add any sugar for me," Siya added, hoping she would notice that she was balancing out the sugar as she walked away in a huff.

When Vaishali walked into Siya's room with a cup of tea on a tray, she saw her flinging clothes angrily into a big plastic bag.

"What happened, Didi? What are you doing with these clothes? Do they have to be dry cleaned?"

"No, they don't," Siya almost yelled.

Placing the cup on the bedside table gingerly, Vaishali backed off timidly. Looking at the terror-stricken expression on Vaishali's face, Siya realised that she was directing her anger and frustration towards this poor girl.

"I'm sorry, Vaishali. It's just that none of my nice clothes are fitting me anymore. All my clothes have become tight. I have nothing to wear to the dinner function this evening…and I'm not in the mood to go shopping for anything new now. When did I become so fat, Vaishali? Why couldn't I have become tall instead?" she scoffed.

Vaishali heaved a sigh of relief. "Didi, you are fine," she said, in a matter-of-fact tone. "There's nothing wrong with how you look. You are fair and pretty. Bhaiyya and you look good together." *This is exactly what my mother-in-law would say. If only Life was that simple.*

"That's not the point, Vaishali. The question is what should I wear this evening so I don't look frumpy and old-fashioned." Vaishali looked thoughtful.

'Why don't you wear a saree, Didi? Remember, the one you wore at Arjun's first birthday party? I can open out the blouse for you…" Her voice trailed off.

That's not a bad idea, Siya. It will camouflage your body fat, while making you look elegant. And, even if you have to leave a few hooks of the blouse open in the front, no one will notice because the pallu will cover it up! The thought cheered her up. "That's a great idea, Vaishali, let me go look for the saree," Siya said, patting Vaishali's face affectionately.

3

That evening, when Samar returned from office and walked into the bedroom, Siya was applying finishing touches to her attire.

"Wow! Saree and all, huh? Who are you trying to impress today?" he asked as he hugged her from behind.

Siya met his gaze in the mirror and beamed at him. *Can this man be so blind? Or, is he naïve? Can't be…then how can he not see that I have put on weight?* "I am trying to impress no one. This is the only outfit that I could fit into today, if you must know," she said, through clenched teeth.

The frustration from the morning loomed, waiting to swoop down on her again. "Oh…then, you should have bought yourself something new to wear. Anyway, I'm glad you are wearing a saree, I rarely get to see you in it since you quit working," Samar pulled away, not noticing the look of anguish on her face. He stood in front of his wardrobe, trying to decide on an outfit, unaware of Siya's mental distress.

"Why would it bother you? You are not the one who put on twenty kilos in nine months so you could give your husband a bonny baby. All you see is the baby who ironically, looks like you, after all the trouble I went through! You don't know how it feels to balloon up suddenly and stay that way. It is so bloody hard…life is so unfair," Siya yelled, storming into the bathroom, banging the door shut. Samar stood motionless, taken aback at Siya's outburst. He did not know what he had said or done to evoke that. Distracting himself, he got ready and was set to go.

Samar was the proverbial Mills & Boon hero—tall, dark and handsome. His eyes—innocent, big and black, framed by long eyelashes, were the most remarkable feature of his face. If you were lucky to have him smiling at you, you could see his dimples at work. His broad shoulders made him look well-built without being overly muscular. Siya, on the other hand, was short, fair, and pretty. With naturally golden-brown hair reaching the middle of her back, she took care to maintain her mane. Her nose was her most striking facial feature—straight and slender. Growing up, it was the one feature, she was mercilessly teased about—her sharp nose. Being inherently introverted only led everyone to assume she was arrogant.

After she came out of the bathroom, Siya took one look in the mirror and was ready to go. Hugging the kids, Samar and Siya kissed them goodnight as they stepped out of their apartment and into the elevator. Samar's expression softened as he looked at Siya. "You look beautiful, Siya."

"You don't have to, Samar," she retorted, avoiding his gaze. When she finally looked up at him, she felt guilty at the love in his eyes. *Why am I punishing him? It's not his fault that I don't fit into my clothes. It's just a society dinner, not the end of the world.* She smiled at him as he reached out and clasped her hand in his.

4

The lawns were beautifully decorated with fairy lights and lanterns all around. As Siya and Samar walked to the venue, they inhaled the fragrance of the desi gulab flowers that had been strewn along the red carpet. Round tables covered in black and gold satin gave the place a regal look. A bar had been set up at one end of the lawn while buffet tables were lined up at the other. Smartly dressed stewards walked around with platters of starters. A cool breeze blew most evenings because of their proximity to the Powai Lake. As it fanned Siya's face, she began to relax. *I'm going to have a good time. Everything looks so beautiful. I'm going to forget how rotten I've felt today.* "Let's get something to drink," she said to Samar, pulling him along towards the bar.

At the bar, she spotted her glamorous neighbours, Naina and Ira. Always together, they were close friends. Siya had met them in passing.

Right after moving into the building six months ago, she had tried to set up play dates with their kids but they had not been forthcoming. Siya's confidence levels were such that this disinterest had discouraged her. To top it all, both Naina and Ira looked like 'yummy mummies'!

Naina was tall, slender, and blessed with 'good' Indian features. With her dusky complexion, long, black hair, she was the kind of girl a man would want to take home to his mother. *I'm sure she has her husband wrapped around her little finger with her looks! Oh Siya, you're being unnecessarily catty!*

Ira, Siya's next door neighbour, on the other hand, looked like a go-getter. Having quit a full-time corporate job, she had become a soft skills trainer. Fair, of medium height and pretty, her hair was always stylishly cut with trendy highlights. Her Facebook wall was plastered with the 'cool' things she said and did. Siya didn't spend much time on Facebook. Although she was friends with both on Facebook—in real life, they hardly acknowledged her—except with a hello. Something that always perplexed Siya. *Why send me a friend request when you look through me in person? Is it because I'm a homemaker and not a driven, career woman? Or, am I just a number to add to your list of friends?*

Siya would never know because she would never have the courage to ask.

As Siya waited for Samar to join her with his drink, she was surprised to see Naina and Ira walking towards her. Siya could see that they were looking her up and down and assessing her saree, jewellery, and makeup. Smiling sweetly, they waved at her like a well-rehearsed chorus. Naina was dressed in a see-through black chiffon saree that lovingly clung to her curves and Ira was wearing a silver, halter-neck dress that showed off her beautifully toned arms, shoulders, and legs. Siya immediately felt stodgy in her silk saree, almost matronly. *What did you expect? You are wearing a camouflage, not a saree, Siya.*

Up close, they looked even more glamorous. Perfect makeup, chic hairdos, beautifully manicured nails—straight out of the pages of a fashion magazine. Samar responded to their greeting as he joined Siya.

"How do you like the set-up, Samar?" Ira asked, in a sweet, lilting voice.

"It's beautiful. Siya and I were just admiring it."

"You know, I have been standing here all evening, giving them instructions on where to put what. Even though they are professionals, they just don't have any aesthetic sense. My legs are hurting from walking around in these heels," she moaned, as she bent down to massage her bare calves, showing off her cleavage. She was fully aware of the effect she was having—Samar was transfixed! Siya was flabbergasted at this blatant flirting. Ira looked up at Samar and he looked away sheepishly. She finally stopped massaging her calves and stood up, smoothening her dress.

As soon as Siya found her voice, she asked Ira where her husband was. "Oh, Kunal is with our son. He is a very hands-on dad—likes to spend all his free time with our son," she said, with a hint of exasperation.

"What about you, Samar, how hands on are you?" she challenged him openly. Samar was so busy staring at her that it took him a few seconds to realise that she was talking to him.

"Well, when I'm not travelling, I spend most of my evenings at home with them."

"Oh, so when do you do the things adults do for fun?" she teased.

"We've been so busy with moving homes and the kids that we haven't been socialising much. Now that we've settled in, we are reclaiming our lives!" Samar replied with a smile that showed off his dimples.

"Oh my God, look at those dimples! As if it's not enough that you are handsome…"

Smiling her sweetest smile, she turned to Siya, "You're a lucky woman—I hope you know that." Making that statement, Ira walked away, leaving behind a grinning Samar and a furious Siya.

Naina stood by quietly, watching this scene. After a few moments of awkward silence, she tried to make conversation by asking if they would be around during the Diwali break. She also invited them to participate in the society's Christmas celebration. Samar said they weren't sure of their holiday plans but would be happy to participate. When the conversation went no further, Naina excused herself, sensing Siya's reserve.

The moment Naina was out of earshot, Samar asked why Siya was being so unfriendly and unresponsive. "Ira was trying to make conversation but you kept throwing her off. And, Naina, when she asked you about the Christmas celebration, couldn't you have said something? No wonder people think you are stuck up," Samar muttered under his breath. Siya couldn't believe that Samar was criticising *her* especially after Ira's behaviour! *And, what about the things she said to me?* she thought. *Telling me I should know how lucky I am that you are married to me? As if, I'm not good enough for you. Or, did you not hear that because you were so busy ogling?* She looked at him mutely. She couldn't trust herself to reply without breaking into tears.

Samar realised the hurt his words had caused. Calming down, he tried to reason with her. He tried to explain that they needed to be friendly with their neighbours. But Siya was so hurt and upset that no words came out. The avalanche of emotions that had been building up inside her since morning threatened to overwhelm her.

Later that night, Siya went over the events of the day. *Just when I'd decided to enjoy myself, those women ruined it. Turning up in their slinky clothing and glamorous hairdos, behaving like it was their private party.* By the time, she had got around to meeting the other neighbours, she had lost the enthusiasm to make conversation and wanted the evening to get over. Fast.

Samar, on the other hand, enjoyed meeting them. Amiable by nature, he was not moody (Men aren't, right?) like Siya. He had tried to rope her into some conversations but Siya had been so reticent that he finally gave up and let her be.

When they came back, Samar tried to reason again with her. "Look, Siya, let it go. How long will you be pissed at what they said? You don't have to socialise with them if you don't want to. Let's just concentrate on developing friendships with people we both like, hmmm? The Malladis, for example. They seemed nice."

Siya wanted to tell him that she was more upset at what *he* had said but she held back. "Okay," she said, instead.

Siya looked at her reflection in the mirror. Dressed in a simple cotton Fabindia nighty, she looked like any other 'housewife'. She hated that term. In her mind, it made her look like her mother—simple, portly, absolutely out of sync with fashion... *I'm not like that. I've travelled abroad, I speak English fluently, my home is well kept, my kids don't speak Hindi all the time, I have all the comforts I want, I cook international cuisines, I read voraciously...all the things Mummy never did. Then, why did it bother me so much when Ira insinuated that Samar is too good for me?* Siya heaved a cold sigh.

5

The thumping lyrics and music of "Girl, look at that body, Girl, look at that body, Girl, look at that body; I work out…" filled the packed gym, raising adrenaline levels.

Siya tried to keep up with the walking pace she had set for herself on the treadmill. A look at the lady on the next treadmill in the mirror dimmed her enthusiasm. Not only was she tall and slim, she was also dressed to show off her flat abs, toned arms, and shapely legs. Siya's insecurities came to the fore again as she thought, *Why do people like her always choose the treadmill next to me? Why do they even come to the gym? Just to rub it in, I guess…* She scoffed at herself. *Run as much as you want, Siya, you'll never look like her. I don't want to. Oh yes, you do! But, you CAN'T. And, you know that.* Her mind had been playing havoc with her all morning. *Nothing I do is ever going to be enough.* She tried to fight it but the pessimist in her won eventually. Feeling discouraged, she got off the treadmill.

The events of last evening had spurred her to hit the gym and increase her cardio time to one hour. But, she had given up at 37 minutes.

She had managed to mask her feelings in front of Samar and the kids that morning. Focussing on what they needed had distracted her. The thought that she'd stopped paying attention to her looks was beginning to bother her. She didn't go shopping for herself at all. Everything centred around the kids, Samar and their home. She wore whatever new clothes Samar bought for her on his travels or what she received as gifts. She used to love shopping.

Siya looked around at the other women working out in the gym. Some of them were attired smartly in fitted racer back tees, slim leggings or capris while others like her had just thrown on the first t-shirt they could lay their hands on along with relaxed fit yoga pants. The hip women were focused on working out to music they were plugged into while the others were totally absorbed in watching shows. Siya loved to watch food shows or comedy channels while walking on the treadmill. It helped to pass time. *Truth be told, I am one of them. Exercise is secondary to me. It's being done just to tick the right boxes. Look at the faces of the other women—tense with concentration as they lift weights and push themselves to run harder, faster.*

She decided to call it a day. *Maybe I'll go for a walk in the park tomorrow. There's no TV there. I will plug in my music and concentrate on walking briskly.*

The music from the gym faded as she rode the elevator down to the ground floor. Walking out of the building, Siya passed by the stores that occupied the ground floor of the commercial complex that housed the gym and many offices atop. An Adidas store had opened up recently. She never ventured into these stores to browse, only when she needed to buy shoes. *No point drooling over stuff that will never suit me,* she thought wryly.

Her mood dived some more when she spotted some women at the Café Coffee Day outlet. All of them looked like they had stepped out of office. *The perks of being a 'working' woman. While we think their life must be so busy, they actually get to sit in a coffee shop at 10 am in their smart work clothes! Look at me, I look bedraggled. Besides, my life is so mundane. Home, shower, breakfast, groceries, plan the menu for lunch/evening snacks/dinner, pick up the kids, their homework, classes, play time... Phew! And, I'm not a 'working' woman.* She bemoaned.

Stop it. Snap out of this, Siya! Isn't that a choice you made? You could have also left your kids with a help and gone off to work. But, you chose to quit work and be with your babies instead. Would you trade that for a salary cheque? No way. Then, make peace with the choices you've made. Or, go find a job! Stop whining.

The display window of Bread Talk had an array of baked goods on display—golden buns, crispy croissants, picture perfect looking bread loaves...*aah, such a treat!* The delicious smells wafting from their bakery drew her inside and she walked into the store and picked up an uncut, rustic loaf of white bread. *A toasted cheese sandwich—that's what I need to pick me up! I'll make it with the delicious pesto gouda cheese I bought from the gourmet food store yesterday. That should help.* Siya thought as she paid for it.

"There is no love greater than the love of food."

Working her way through the grilled pesto cheese sandwich later, Siya's spirits affirmed that thought. Standing at the dining room window, she gazed at the buildings surrounding Solitaire—Brentwood, Florentine, Eternia, Birchwood. They stood like sentinels, reminding her of Manhattan, with its tightly packed sky scrapers. The crisp exterior of the sandwich contrasted beautifully with the creaminess of the luscious, oozing cheese as she bit in. The subtle freshness of the pesto lifted the veil of despair that had settled over her heart. Thankfully, their apartments were not matchbox sized and built to allow in plenty of natural light and cross ventilation. Feeling positively charged, Siya decided to get on with her day. A round to the supermarket was due as groceries had to be replenished. Siya looked up the list drawn by Vaishali, cross-checked if something else needed to be added and walked out.

Waiting in the corridor for the elevator to arrive, Siya wondered if she would bump into any of her neighbours from last night. In hindsight, she felt sheepish about not mingling with the others. *They must really think I'm anti-social! I'll just have to apologise and tell them how my migraine was bothering me. But, you don't suffer from migraine, Siya! Shhhh…* Siya and Samar lived on the nineteenth floor which meant that the lift made a lot of stops before it reached the ground floor. Every time it stopped, Siya got tense. Gradually, the elevator filled with people—a couple from the tenth floor, maids, delivery boys, the building plumber… Phew! Siya exhaled as she exited the elevator. *All clear.*

Forty-five minutes later, Siya handed her grocery bags to Ashok, their driver. "*Aap ye lekar ghar jao. Main walk karoongee.*" She had decided to take a detour for a change and do some window shopping in the nearby galleries. Although it was only a 10 minute walk from home, it could turn into an expensive one! She had always loved to see the wares on display. Apparel, jewellery, sarees, handbags, shoes, décor pieces, knick knacks for the home, kids' clothes and toys, linen—from all over the country—were proudly showcased at these galleries—their target being the homemaker.

An ethnic, printed tunic on display in one of the windows attracted her attention. She stepped into the shop. It was a small rectangular space, with racks on both sides of the wall. In the middle was a long table where one could keep items that had been selected. At the end of the racks, there were two cubicles for use as trial rooms.

On the opposite side, a tall lady and presumably her friend were going through the hangers. They were whispering to each other, discussing the designs and colour combinations. Both of them were dressed in jeans and Anokhi tops. *Hmmm...skinny jean-clad women everywhere I go,* thought Siya. She tried hard to ignore them and concentrate on the clothes but there was something familiar—their voice? Manners?

The women turned around to face the rack beside which Siya stood. She gaped openly at their faces. The shorter lady gave her a polite smile. Siya continued to stare. *Could it be her? The voice sounds like hers. But, it's been ages. She used to be pleasantly plump. Could it be her? This one is slim!*

"Aisha?" she asked, hesitantly.

The taller lady stared back at her for a few seconds. Siya waited...sheepishly. A smile began to form on the lady's lips and slowly travelled to her eyes, lighting them up. "Siya! O my God, it's you! What a surprise!" she shrieked, enveloping her in a warm hug.

"How are you? When did you move to Mumbai? Where have you been all these years?" Aisha fired one question after another in an accented voice.

"You're looking fabulous, Aisha. You have lost so much weight! I wasn't sure it's you!" Siya laughed and hugged her back warmly.

"Thank you! What happened to you? I thought you would always remain petite like a doll."

Siya felt a prick of emotion at Aisha's observation and lowered her eyes. She didn't know how to respond.

"Hi! I'm Rajni. I've heard so much about you from Aisha. She always talks of you fondly," said her companion, extending her hand warmly, to undo some of the hurt Aisha's comment had caused. Siya had never seen kinder eyes. She smiled back.

Rajni continued, "Aisha, is that something you say to a dear friend after so many years? Very bad!"

Aisha's smile faded as the insensitivity of her remark dawned on her. Grabbing both of Siya's hands in her palms, Aisha squeezed them warmly. "Siya, that's not how I meant it. It's been more than fifteen years since I last saw you... the pictures of you just flashed in front of my eyes! I'm so sorry."

"Don't be silly. The Aisha I knew wouldn't hurt a fly if she could help it. It doesn't look like she has changed much." Siya beamed at her, having pushed the hurt away.

"Let's meet for coffee soon. There's so much to talk about! Give me your number. I will call you later," said Aisha. Aisha and Siya exchanged numbers and parted ways, after making plans to meet.

Delhi, July 1991

We've only just begun—Carpenters

"You better straighten out, baby,"—this refrain had been playing in my mind that morning. Where had it come from? A song by George Michael? Bryan Adams? Or, was it a dialogue from Top Gun*? And then I remembered—it was the telephone call from the previous night...*

Everyone else had gone to bed when the phone rang at 10 pm. I answered it not knowing who to expect and had been pleasantly surprised at the male voice on the other side, speaking fluent English. You see, in Delhi, Hindi was then the preferred language of the milieu. From my neighbourhood friends to their parents, from my schoolmates to the teachers—everyone spoke in Hindi. Even though the medium of instruction in my school was English, we were taught pidgin English! It really used to get my goat.

In all my years of living in Delhi, I hadn't come across anyone who was comfortable with English. Also, my neighbourhood was inhabited mostly by traders and small-time businessmen, government employees, middle-income group...you get the drift? While the business class was more interested in multiplying their money, the mid-income groups were keen on saving it. No one was intent on improving their English.

My Dad had been employed in the Middle East when I was younger—you know, the middle class dream to work abroad and earn foreign currency which would translate into savings later. My early schooling there had aligned me towards the language and I was fluent in it. Moving to Delhi from the Middle East had been a rude shock in many ways...but, I digress.

When I heard the male voice on the other end of the phone speak in English, confidently, and without hesitation, I was surprised. And, impressed.

I'm trying to recall the conversation word for word. "Hi. I've seen you around. I'd like to be friends with you." I was tempted to reply "Yes"! After all, I didn't get propositioned in English every day! But I couldn't be that forward; only "fast" girls were forward. I replied what any eighteen-year-old girl, from a middle-class family, studying in an all girls' college should,

"No, I am not interested."

"Why not? You think you're too good?" he had asked.

"Yes," I had answered, simply because I could not think of anything else!

"Well, you better straighten out, baby," he said as he hung up the phone!

Nobody hangs up on a girl, especially if you are trying to befriend her. You cajole and plead with flattery, even beg if you think she may come around. You don't hang up on a girl. That's a cardinal sin... you cannot flout the unspoken law of the universe! This was also the reason why the conversation stayed with me. I caught myself smiling as I thought about it. "Thank God he's English speaking! Those I-want-to-friendship-with-you types are so off putting!" And I wondered if he'd ever call again.

6

Siya could not focus on the rest of her shopping expedition, despite the wide array of products on display. Bold pendants, gypsy style earrings, bracelets, bangles, broad and intricately designed amulets, necklaces encrusted with gemstones...everything that she simply loved looking at!

Meeting one's best friend after fifteen years is like travelling back in a time machine. Flashbacks from the past kept buzzing around in her head. Memories that had been relegated to a corner of her heart came flooding back. From her childhood, to becoming teenagers and then adulthood. Aisha was a part of her past.

Walking back home, she reminisced their years together in school. Siya was eleven years old when she joined St. Mary's School in Safdarjung Enclave, a posh locality in South Delhi. Aisha's mother had passed away that year. There had been a lot of speculation about how she had died. Some said she'd committed suicide, while others believed she had had a heart attack. Siya felt sorry for Aisha and wanted to reach out and hug her... *Losing one's mother must be difficult,* she had thought. That's how they had become close friends.

Over the next two years, they spent a lot of time together, sharing every little thing with each other; their hopes, dreams, secrets—during school and after. Aisha's family comprised of her two sisters, her father, and her Naani. Aisha's elder sister was reserved but sweet. Aisha's younger sister was autistic and needed special attention.

Naani was very loving—even towards Siya. Back then, Aisha had nursed a crush over a schoolmate since kindergarten. She had been in love with him for a long, long time... But, she had never expressed her feelings as she was chubby and self-conscious! *I must remember to ask her about him. Does she know where he is or what he's doing? She used to be so crazy about him,* Siya smiled as she recalled.

While Aisha was a talented, spirited girl, Siya was the quieter, prettier one. A lot of boys who were friendly with Aisha would ask her to set them up on a date with Siya. What fun they used to have discussing those silly boys and their corny lines! Siya was a dreamer who would dabble in poetry. Aisha was always the first one to read her poems and say something nice and encouraging!

Two years later, Siya changed schools. After that, Aisha and Siya kept in touch for a while—on the phone. Gradually, they became more absorbed in their studies, and lost track of the other's life. Ultimately, they just became a name with a phone number in a telephone diary.

Although Aisha had attended Siya's wedding, they hardly got a chance to talk in private. Siya moved to another city soon after and once again, they lost touch. Email, online chatting, social media were all in their nascent phase then and STD calls were expensive. Siya never found a friend like Aisha. Of course, she had her work colleagues but that lasted only until she had her babies. She quit her job soon after. Then, it was just her and them.

Bumping into Aisha at the gallery was fortuitous—she was being given a chance to renew a cherished friendship. While she was looking forward to that, there was a nagging thought at the back of her head. Aisha was now slim and sexy whereas Siya was not as petite as she used to be. She had changed. Could she handle that? She was used to being the more desirable one!

"Hi, Siya!" Naina waved at her as she was returning from the park with the kids later that evening. *Oh no...* Signalling Vaishali to take them home, she turned to face Naina.

"Hi, Naina! How are you?"

"I'm not good. I'm feeling so fat and bloated after the party last night. I had two glasses of wine and dessert too. I need to work it off in my power yoga class now," Naina moaned as her hands roamed over her flat abdomen and curvaceous waist. *First world problems,* Siya sighed. "You don't need to, Naina. You're blessed with a slim figure and great height. Party on!"

"Aah, there's Ira!" Naina announced, smiling sweetly at Siya.

Looking as fit as a yoga instructor, Ira approached them, giving Siya a cold look. *Eye shadow and nude lipstick for yoga class? Boy, oh boy*! Siya could not contain the bitchy thoughts. "How are you today, Siya? You guys left early last night. You should have stayed and joined us on the dance floor. I'm sure Samar likes to shake a leg..." Ira cooed, her voice dripping with honey. Siya stiffened. She was beginning to dislike this woman.

"Samar had an early morning meeting," she answered, as pleasantly as she could.

"It was a fun evening, *na*? People were wowed!" Naina announced, smugly. "So many people came and congratulated us. It was so rewarding. *Hai na,* babe?" Ira, who was busy checking her makeup in a hand-held mirror, nodded indulgently at Naina. Siya was puzzled at this display of mutual admiration. The conversation continued, mainly between Naina and Ira.

"You know what? We should have a kitty!" squealed Naina. "You know, where us ladies get to meet and know each other. There are so many new people in the building now. We could take turns to host it, start with coffee mornings where the hostess can serve tea/coffee along with high fibre, low calorie snacks. What do you say, Siya?" *High fibre, low calorie?* "I think we could rope in some husbands too, if we organise them on Sunday mornings. We could play some games as an ice-breaker. I can conduct some games that I use in my training programs. It will be fun!" continued Ira. Siya nodded meekly. *They are full of ideas on how to torture other people for their own enjoyment!*

"Hey, please let me know if you'll be here in December. We are planning a Christmas celebration. You must participate," trilled Naina, trying to catch her reflection in the glass of the notice board in the elevator lobby.

"It's too early to tell, Naina. Besides, what can I possibly do? Both of you are good at these things, I'm sure you don't need me," Siya replied.

They looked at each other and smiled knowingly. "Of course, we will be the heart of the show but there will be so many things to do! It would be nice to not have to do it all yourself, you know. You could be part of the support staff," Ira quipped with a cheeky smile.

"We are getting late for our class, girl, let's go!" yelled Naina and dragged Ira away.

The duo walked out of the building, leaving Siya seething, again. *Support staff...how can she even say something like that? She will treat me like a spot boy! Make me fetch her coffee, her dry cleaning, her kid and what not…like Meryl Streep in* The Devil Wears Prada. *I'm not going to be her errand girl.* She decided not to mention this to Samar. He would advise her to get more involved in social activities. Siya was sure that he would not understand how she struggled to cope with her insecurities and negative self-image.

She spent the rest of the evening alone, calming her frayed nerves, finding solace in music (the radio) and books (a copy of Gulzar's poems). Music and books always helped. As tears welled up in her eyes, she wondered why Ira singled her out to poke gibes at. And, why did she let it affect her? Why couldn't she just ignore them and carry on?

Siya tried to quieten her thoughts by staring out of the window and taking in the Powai Lake. The reflection of the surrounding hills on its calm surface, the greenery that bordered the lake right from the IIT campus and all around like an emerald necklace, the palm trees that stood by guarding its tranquillity…until she felt composed and the negative thoughts had subsided. Just then, the door opened quietly and her little one peered in. She looked up and smiled at him, opening her arms wide. He rushed in to hug her. Enveloping him in her arms, she smiled.

7

The following week, Siya received a text message from Aisha.

"Free to meet for coffee at eleven?"

"Yes! Do you know where Aromas is?"

"Yes, I've seen it."

"Great. I'll meet you there. Ciao."

I must remember to ask her about that guy she had a crush on. What was his name? She used to be mad about him, Siya mused, as she dressed in a navy-blue top with jeans. *Dark colours are slimming*. The jeans were a tad tight. *I'm not going to eat anything so I should be okay. Should I wear my Spanx? It'll help contract my stomach. Yeah, I think I'll do that.* She rummaged through the drawer in which she stored her undergarments. It was lying tucked away in a corner, unused and almost brand new.

After five minutes of holding her breath in as she tried to pull it up her legs, Siya exhaled in relief. *Oh gosh, this is hard work.* She pulled the Spanx up till it sat below her bust. *Hmmpphh*...the Spanx contracted the fat of her torso from the bust line till her thighs. Siya smiled at her reflection.

Ecstatic at the slimming effect, she put on some accessories and was all set for the outing. She observed herself critically in the mirror just before leaving—full front and then, in profile. *Do I still look fat? Hmmm...let's see what Aisha says.*

After her run in with Ira the other day, Siya waited for the elevator warily. She didn't want to be roped into another conversation about social events. With her eyes glued to the elevator display and ears tuned to any sounds from the flat next door, Siya rushed into the lift as it opened and jabbed at the Close Door button. She was looking forward to meeting Aisha and didn't want any nastiness to puncture her enthusiasm. As soon as she got to the ground floor, she hurried out and heaved a sigh of relief, only after she walked out of the main gate. *Phew! Relax, Siya, breathe in, breathe out... Relax.*

The walk to the coffee shop was hardly fifteen minutes from her apartment. Walking through the leafy by-lanes of Hiranandani, she passed by many people she recognised. School mums, former neighbours (she'd lived in the township for five years, even though she had moved to Solitaire recently), gym members, friends of friends, people from the bank. It was very familiar and comforting.

Aisha was already waiting outside Café Aromas when Siya got there. Tall (five feet six inches), clear complexioned with shoulder-length straight hair (*she used to have such frizzy hair in school!*), Aisha was very attractive. *Wow, she is quite a head turner*! *How did she lose so much weight?* They hugged warmly when they met and proceeded to a table inside the café.

At the café, Aisha ordered a herbal concoction, Yogi Chai, while Siya settled for a chocolate milkshake. Aisha's chai came in a dainty infusion pot along with a healthy-looking cookie on the side. Siya's milkshake came in a mason jar with a generous dollop of whipped cream and a cherry on top. *Hmmm, no wonder she's so slim...look at your drink! What a glutton you are.* Siya immediately regretted ordering it, feeling fat and uncomfortable as her Spanx started rolling down her stomach.

Picking up her spoon, she started scooping the cream off her milkshake and putting it on a side plate. "What are you doing? That's the best part!" Aisha said, incredulously.

"I forgot to tell them that I didn't want it... I don't like whipped cream," Siya replied. *Liar. You love whipped cream. You love anything that's sweet. Who are you trying to fool?* "My boys generally love to have the cream when I order this," she said, even as she recalled the reluctance with which she would share it with them.

"My boys love it, too! What a coincidence that we both have boys! How old are yours?" Aisha asked.

"They are seven and four."

"Mine are twelve and ten. We should get them together some time."

Siya nodded as she took a sip of her milkshake, relishing the chocolatey gooeyness.

"I'm so happy I bumped into you, Siya! This is the best thing to come out of moving to Mumbai," Aisha said, squeezing her hand affectionately.

Siya smiled brightly. "Right back at you, Aisha. Where have you moved from? Delhi?"

"We moved to the US after marriage. My husband is an investment banker. We met at work before he was posted abroad. He sent a proposal through his family. We were in the US for seven years."

"Aah, that explains the slight accent! Why did you move back so soon? People generally don't return after having lived abroad."

"Yea, he did well and got promoted in good time too," she paused, "but things are getting bad there. Lots of banks are downsizing and laying people off. In hindsight, he feels it was a prudent move. He's in a good place now and the timing couldn't have been better."

"Hmmm, that's great! What about you? What have you been doing? You were so full of fantastic ideas back in school," Siya wanted to know more.

Aisha smiled wryly.

"After college, Papa wanted to see me settled as soon as possible. He kept saying that's what my Mom would have wanted had she been alive. He said I could do whatever I wanted after that. I had started working after college and I would have liked to continue but suitable marriage proposals were not easy to come by. Papa got me married at the earliest. Thankfully, he was not a total stranger. He was well-educated and came from a good family. I couldn't have gotten a better husband, in Papa's opinion. I struggled hard to get a working visa after moving to the US but it never came through. It was really frustrating. To pass my time, I took distance learning courses and studied some more. My husband was eager to start a family but it wasn't easy for me. You remember how chubby I was. We had to undergo some tests before starting treatment. It was a highly stressful time for me and I put on more weight. Fortunately, the treatment worked and we had our first son. But, by then I ballooned up even more. I went into postpartum depression. To get over that, I started hitting the gym in frustration. Lost some of it. Had another baby and put on more weight. Went back to the gym with a vengeance. I changed my lifestyle, my eating habits... I transformed myself since I couldn't change any other damn thing!"

"Wow!" Siya exclaimed when Aisha stopped. "You did good, Aisha. I'm really proud of you. You must be so happy!" she said, squeezing her hand.

Aisha laughed cynically. "If losing weight alone could bring happiness, then I would be the happiest person alive!" she added, with a wry smile.

I would be really happy if I could look like her right now! Siya thought.

"Are you not happy, Aisha?" she asked in earnest.

"Of course I am, you silly girl, I was just trying to sound worldly...you're so cute," Aisha laughed. "Your turn now! Tell me what's been happening in your life, Siya."

"My life? Well, pretty much the same as yours. Graduated from college, worked in hotels for a bit, met my husband. Got married at twenty-three, moved a couple of cities, continued working and waited for five years before having our first child."

"Why?" Aisha asked. "I mean, did you have problems conceiving?"

Siya hesitated. "Not really. I wasn't ready. I'm not a child friendly person, you see. Having said that, motherhood changed me. I quit working after my son was born. I wanted to be with my darling boy. I couldn't bear to leave him in anyone else's care; I enjoyed watching him grow. What's more, I wanted another baby! Now, I'm a full-time homemaker, mom, wife...no ambition to make money or have a scintillating career. I read, write, shop, eat...as is evident from the amount of weight I've put on since," Siya chuckled.

Aisha smiled in understanding. "Siya, I'm sorry about the weight remark I made the other day. It's just that I couldn't believe... I always picture you as this pretty perfect best friend I had in school. I didn't mean to hurt you. God promise!" Aisha said, clutching the skin of her throat with her fingers solemnly. Siya burst out laughing. That single gesture brought back so many good old memories!

"Well, I did feel bad but I will say this—I know you didn't mean to hurt me." Aisha heaved a sigh of relief.

"Come to think of it, a couple of recent incidents are really making me think about it," Siya continued.

"About what, Siya? What incidents?"

"After meeting you that day, Aisha, I went back home and looked at my old photographs, some recent ones too. It hit me hard only then... I have put on a lot of weight. But no one ever pointed it out. When I look in the mirror, I still see the same girl I've seen for the past so many years. I don't notice the flab or the dark circles or the stray grey hair... It's just me."

"Oh, Siya," said Aisha, grasping her hand. "You will always be the same girl! Honest, loyal, loving, fun to hang out with. You were my only friend growing up... Please stay this way. What's more, if you lose weight, you'll have all the men running after you while I will again be standing by, all alone, watching the stampede!" Siya burst into laughter as Aisha beamed at her.

"Aah, lemme enjoy the picture that conjures up in my mind," Siya said, wistfully. "Who am I kidding? If I can get my husband to start looking at me instead of a screen then it will be worthwhile," Siya added, wryly.

"Hmmm...trouble in paradise?" Aisha asked. Siya rolled her eyes in mock exasperation.

The conversation continued as they brought each other up to date on the happenings in their lives—their siblings, family, husbands, kids, in-laws, teachers, school mates, Mumbai...and soon they were giggling teenagers again!

"Huh, it's one-thirty already!" exclaimed Siya, as she looked at her watch finally. "I have to pick up my little one from school. Sorry, but I have to go."

"Of course! That's okay. We'll keep meeting now," said Aisha, standing as she retrieved her handbag from the adjoining chair. That's when Siya noticed the appreciative glances that were directed at Aisha as they walked out of the café. *I used to be the one getting those glances. How the tables have turned…*

"Oh, by the way, Aisha, what happened to that boy you had a huge crush on? What was his name?" Siya asked, casually.

Aisha stopped in her tracks. "Boy? Which boy? I had a crush on so many…that's the only thing I could do then!" she answered with a smile.

"*Arrey*, that one you liked since nursery! The one you used to almost stalk in school. Didn't you two get together for a bit in college?" Siya thought she saw a flicker of recognition on Aisha's face briefly.

"I don't know who you're talking about," said Aisha, in a cold, emphatic tone. Siya couldn't believe that. *Really? She couldn't stop obsessing about him then! How could she have forgotten?* She didn't think it wise to pursue the topic. As she enveloped Aisha in a hug, she sensed a perceptible change in her demeanour.

"Take care, Aisha. See you again, real soon," said Siya, as they parted.

As Siya walked away from Aisha, she wondered why her tone had changed suddenly. *Did something happen between them? Or, am I reading too much into it? If I remember correctly, she told me that they were seeing each other when she came to our wedding…how did that end? Not well, I guess.*

At the school, as she waited to pick up her little one, she bumped into Paru, a dear friend, whom she had known since they had first moved to Hiranandani. They had been neighbours in the previous building, Sovereign. Paru was a simple Gujarati woman who came from a rich business family. Although she mostly wore simple cotton clothes, she loved to match everything from her nail paint to hair accessories to her handbag! When you set eyes on Paru's sandals, you'd know what the rest of her outfit would be like. Siya always delighted in this quirk!

"Hi, Paru! It's so good to see you. What brings you to school at this hour of the day? Don't your boys walk back home?" she asked.

"Hi, Siya, I'm not here for the kids. I'm here to meet the head of the pre-primary section for a job." Paru answered with a smile.

"Aah, that's why you're dressed in formal colours today! You are so good with kids; I'm sure you'll get the job," Siya smiled. It was then that she looked at Paru again, in totality, from head to toe. "Paru, you have lost a lot of weight! I thought there was something different. You look great! How did you do it? Please tell me the secret." Siya pleaded, her tone yo-yoing from surprise to admiration. Paru beamed back.

"I'm consulting a dietician, Ambika Nair. I've lost five kilos in two months! I didn't think I would be able to do it but she is amazing!" answered Paru, with apparent glee.

"Wow, five kilos—really? That is fantastic. How does it work, Paru? Does she starve you? Does she make you eat only salads and boiled vegetables? Do you feel hungry all the time?" Siya had a whole lot of questions.

"Easy, Siya, easy. I'll answer your questions one by one," Paru spent the next five minutes explaining the diet recommended by her dietician. She also told her about the exercise regimen she followed. Diligently, making mental notes, Siya had some follow-up questions which Paru answered patiently. Siya asked Paru if she could share her dietician's number. Now, Paru was forced to lose weight due to health issues. Consequently, she couldn't understand why Siya was so conscious about her figure and wanted to lose weight. Siya had no answer. She couldn't very well say that she felt obese and obsolete when she met fitter women and how that affected her confidence. Especially because her husband looked at these fitter, glam women with admiring glances.

Siya made some lame excuse, linking it to ill-health. As they bid goodbye to each other, Paru promised to send Siya the dietician's number.

8

True to her word, Paru sent her the dietician's number later that evening. Siya immediately messaged Ambika and waited for her reply. The next morning, she still hadn't heard from Ambika. As she walked to the gym, after Samar and the kids had left, she was self conscious. Unhappy about how she looked and unable to come to terms with it, she constantly compared herself to the girls and ladies she passed by along with the svelte babes leaving the gym!

Once inside, other than the usual faces, she spotted Aisha doing weights and walked up to her. Dressed in a red, racer-back tee and well-fitted black leggings, she was looking super sexy. "Aisha, hi!"

"Hi, Siya! I didn't know you are a member here."

"It doesn't show on me, *na*?" Siya said in a self-deprecating tone.

"I didn't mean it that way! I thought you'd forgiven me for my boo-boo, Siya," Aisha remarked, making a sad face.

"Forgiven and forgotten! You know, I'm planning to go on a diet. A friend of mine, Paru, has lost weight, after consulting a dietician. I've just messaged her!"

"That's great, Siya! I'm so glad you are taking a step in the right direction. I've met so many people who just crib and crib but don't do anything about it."

"Aisha, I don't know if I'll be able to do it but I'd definitely like to give it a try."

"Of course, you will. If I can do it then so can you! I'm always here if you need any help," she said, smiling warmly.

"I know. *Chalo*, you carry on with your workout. I will get on with mine. See you later."

As she worked out, Siya chided herself for blurting out everything to Aisha. Wondering what Aisha would think if she couldn't stick with it and lose weight, she felt her enthusiasm waning.

After freshening up, post workout, when she checked her phone she had a message from Ambika asking her to call at seven that evening.

Siya spent the whole day being mindful, watching what she ate and wondering whether to inform Samar about her dieting plans. She didn't want him telling her that she was fine as she was and didn't need to lose any weight. "Just eat sensibly, exercise regularly and you'll be fine," was probably what he would say. He would never understand that she was not okay with being "just fine" any more.

More than the snide comments of Ira on her physical appearance, it was meeting with Aisha that had shaken her up. She couldn't believe how Aisha had transformed at first. Later, when Aisha narrated the details of how she had lost the excessive weight through sheer determination and focus, Siya felt in awe of her. And, a bit sheepish.

Here was her friend, who had managed to accomplish the impossible despite lack of any help. She'd managed the babies, her home and achieved her goals. It inspired her. Siya was fortunate to have ample resources in terms of help...but, the thought had never struck her. She had no goals or aspirations for herself. Her life would just pass by if she didn't challenge herself in some way.

Would Samar understand that she needed this for herself more than anyone else?

9

Siya called Ambika at the appointed time and spoke to her for nearly 45 minutes. Ambika asked for a whole lot of information, based on which she would send a detailed diet plan by email. Siya was exhausted—she had not spoken about herself with anyone for so long. She was relieved to share her anxieties with an expert albeit a bit apprehensive, as to whether it would work.

Her boys returned from the park soon thereafter and excitedly narrated an incident that had occurred there with a stray dog. The evening passed by with the retelling and enactment of the same incident in front of Samar at dinner time. When Samar asked where Siya had been then, Aryan mentioned that Mama had an important phone call at home. Siya tried shushing him but Samar's curiosity had been triggered. She haltingly mentioned her conversation with the dietitian recommended by Paru. Samar listened briefly but, as expected, fired a volley of questions that she couldn't dodge.

Siya got irritated. Questions irked her, because she would have to answer them. She would have to string together her thoughts and feelings into words. She could not get away with giving Samar superficial answers. She would have to be candid which meant that she would have to share some of her insecurities.

"Paru has lost five kilos in two months on her plan. Her plan includes a whole lot of grains, seeds and alternate flours, no pills. She has to avoid some things like sugar and, she needs to exercise alongside." Siya's voice trailed off as she tried answering.

"That's common sense, Siya. You don't need a dietician to tell you that."

"Its common sense, Mama," repeated Aryan, trying to imitate his dad, much to her chagrin. Siya stared at him so hard that he went quiet.

"No, Samar, it's not common sense alone. It requires some level of knowledge and experience backed by extensive research. When your clients show positive results based on the same, then you know you're doing it right," Siya added, with a little more conviction. "Do you know she is asking me to include a lot of natural foods to aid weight loss that I wasn't even aware of? Things like barley water, buttermilk, white pumpkin juice, wheat bran…besides eliminating dals for a while."

"No dals? That's strange. Aren't they a major source of proteins for vegetarians?" Samar asked, keen to understand what Siya was getting into.

"Yes! But, not the way we cook it," Siya answered animatedly, eager to explain the logic that was shared with her by Ambika. "Initially, I will have to stay away from dals but she'll introduce it back later, once I show results." Samar was a tough nut to crack but Siya tried her best. He didn't seem convinced.

She finally tried to appease him emotionally. "Despite working out so regularly, I'm not losing any weight…it's really frustrating." She banged the table with one hand, exasperated with the effort of trying to make him see sense in it. Dinner time turned sombre. The kids looked from Siya to Samar and back. Were their parents having a fight? Was Mama going to shout ? Was Papa upset with her?

"Siya, I will never stop you from doing anything if it means so much to you. I just want to ensure you don't waste your effort and money on a hopeless cause. If you've done your research and find this approach worth trying then go ahead. Just make sure we are not deprived of our dose of junk from time to time!" Samar said, lightening the mood around the table immediately!

10

Ambika sent the diet plan next morning. It was five pages long. Siya spent the morning going through it in detail and making notes. She found it daunting but still planned for it. Luckily, she had the ingredients required for breakfast on Day 1, so she plunged into it!

After eating a bowl of oats cooked in milk, she was sceptical if it would sustain her till lunch. Years ago, she had tried the General Motors diet and given up on Day 1 because it was too difficult. This time, she'd resolved to try harder. Mid-morning and lunch on Day 1 passed quickly and successfully. It was post lunch that the craving began. She was so hooked to a 'little treat' after lunch that she started becoming increasingly frustrated and anxious. By tea time, the frustration receded when she had two Marie biscuits with her tea.

To overcome her anxiety and channelise her thoughts elsewhere, she decided to head to the gym. Ever since her weight had been playing on her mind, she had gotten into the habit of watching her reflection in the display windows of the shops on her way to the gym. *Am I looking less bloated? Could be…what nonsense! It's not even been a day.* She chided herself, looking away from her reflection. *Time to find my trainer and tell him that I will not need his services for a while. I have to do this on my own steam…*

The loud music blaring from the speakers belted out Gloria Gaynor's classic 'I will survive', setting the mood for a workout session. As Siya looked around at the crowd, the aptness of the song dawned on her. The evening crowd of fitness enthusiasts was diametrically opposite from the morning crowd. While the morning crowd consisted of middle-aged homemakers and business people, the evening lot comprised mainly of youngsters, college goers, some high school kids, young professionals, and the occasional senior corporate professional. Looking at the way they were dressed, Siya felt like she was on the sets of a Karan Johar film. Trendy workout clothes, hip cell phones, latest audio accessories, naturally slim and toned bodies. *Age has not touched them,* Siya sighed. *What are they here for? They obviously don't need to lose any weight.*

Siya sucked her stomach in as she spotted her trainer, Ajay, at the other end of the floor, deep in conversation with a curvaceous young woman. She walked towards him, not looking at herself in the mirrors that lined the wall. Instead, she focused on the object of Ajay's attention. *Something about her is very familiar. Probably some model!*

"Hi, Ajay."

"Hello, ma'am, how come you're here in the evening today? *Aap toh subah aatey ho,*" he said by way of acknowledgement.

The woman speaking to Ajay turned around to face Siya—it was Ira. Siya squirmed, self-consciously.

"Hello, Siya. I didn't know Ajay was *your* trainer. I will have to think again about training with him now," she said, smiling sweetly at both of them.

"Don't worry, Ira ma'am. Siya ma'am works out in the morning. I can train you in the evening. It will not upset her schedule," he said smugly, the gibe totally lost on him.

Siya hastily looked away from Ira and turned to Ajay. "I need to speak with you for a minute."

"Ma'am, excuse me, I'll be back; stay here," he said reluctantly, looking at Ira, completely smitten. She just shrugged her shoulders, nonchalantly.

As he stepped away from her, Siya informed him that she was on a diet and hence won't be working out with weights for a while as her dietician wanted her to do only cardio for some time.

"*Arrey*, ma'am, why did you have to consult dietician outside. We are here, no? Just eat as I say and continue to work out with me," he urged.

"Ajay, I've been listening to you for one year now. I have lost only three kilos! That's like a drop in the ocean. I need to lose at least fifteen more. I've already got a plan in place. Once I achieve my goal, I'll be back. I just thought I should let you know," said Siya, looking over his shoulder to see if anyone was listening in.

"Ok, ma'am. But, after you lose weight, you'll start again, *na*? Then, you will need to get toned to look sexy like her," he said with a wink, nodding in Ira's direction. Siya got bugged and walked towards the nearest empty treadmill. She tried to understand why she was being so testy and figured it could be because of the lack of food.

An hour later, as she walked home from the gym, tired and sweaty, she thought of the meal that awaited her. Grilled chicken, bajra roti, and salad. That didn't sound bad. As she walked into the building, she spotted Naina and Ira, strolling around. *Oh God, not them again.*

"Hey, Siya! Wait up," called out Naina as Siya kept walking the other way, pretending she hadn't seen or heard her. Naina ran to catch up with her. "Hi!" she said, looking fabulously fit in calf length white capris with a printed halter neck top that showed off her toned shoulders and arms.

Do they dress like this every day? Don't they have any 'normal' clothes in their wardrobe? Siya wondered. "Hi! What's the matter, Naina? All ok?" she asked.

"Yes, yes. I'm ok. Ira and I were talking about organising the first kitty sometime next week. Are you free on Wednesday?"

In the meanwhile, Ira had walked up to them. She stood by listening. "I'm not free on Wednesday, Naina," Siya replied, trying not to offend her.

"How about Friday then?" Ira enquired, with an ingratiating smile.

Siya couldn't understand why they were hell-bent on having her in the kitty. She pursed her lips, giving the impression that she was thinking hard about her plans for Friday. "I'm sorry, Friday doesn't work either."

"Really? Does it clash with your diet?" asked Ira, with an irritating, know-it-all smile. Siya was taken aback. *How did she know? Oh, that silly smitten trainer must have told her… men just don't know what to keep to themselves.*

"What diet, Siya?" Naina asked with interest.

"Oh, it's just something I've started." Siya tried to brush it aside as unimportant. "Coming back to Friday, I have a PTM in school which generally takes a few hours. I'll join in if it finishes in good time. Ok?" she asked, in a conciliatory tone.

"Sure. I'll keep you posted," Naina smiled back as Ira looked on.

"Sorry, Naina, but I have to go now," Siya said as she scampered towards the elevator before they could make another suggestion. Siya could not understand why Ira enjoyed troubling her.

When Samar got home that evening, he wanted to know more about her diet. "So, how was the first day? Easy?

Hard? Very hard?" he asked, observing her face for any signs.

"Well…it was not as bad as I had imagined. I'm not feeling starved or dizzy with hunger despite having exercised for forty-five minutes. I managed to eat pretty much everything that's been listed down; just dinner left to finish for the day!" Siya answered with satisfaction.

"How much did you cheat? Tell me that," asked Samar, with a naughty glint in his eyes. He knew she had a weakness for chocolates and all things sweet.

"Not a bit. I was tempted to but I didn't. God alone knows how I managed that," she replied.

Later that night, she told Samar about Naina and Ira's kitty party invitation. "What did you say?" he asked.

"I told them I couldn't make it as I have something else that day." He looked up from his game and turned to face her. Siya resisted the urge to tell him how Ira had wanted to recruit Siya as support staff for their event. "What? It's the truth! Besides, I'm not the kitty type—you know that," she said, defensively.

"That's it? You just said you couldn't make it?" he asked, an edge of irritation in his voice.

"No, I told them I have a PTA in school and I'll join in if it finishes in time," she answered, with a measure of conviction, looking him in the eye. *She decided not to tell him about her meeting with Ira at the gym either. She didn't want to be told that it was her own insecurities that made her react that way. She did not want the mirror to be shown to her face.*

"I thought you wanted to know your neighbours better. It would be a good opportunity to make friends." Samar argued.

"Of course I do; but not with people who enjoy kitties!"

"Siya, kitty is just a term associated with the meet-ups women have without their husbands."

"That term rankles me. Just like 'housewife'," she added, making air quotes for housewife. Samar rolled his eyes. "I won't have anything in common with that kind of crowd. I'd like to know people who I can have conversations with about the things that matter!" she argued.

"Matter? Conversations that matter? Like what? World politics? Economic sanctions? Human rights violations?" Samar sneered. Siya looked at him, eyes blazing with anger and hurt.

"You are being closed in your thoughts..." Samar pointed out.

Siya sighed. "It's okay, Samar. I know I can't have conversations about finance or politics or even sports. But, I do enjoy books and music and theatre and a whole lot of other things! Maybe, I am being closed but that's because of the vibe I get from them."

"You're reading too much into this. Don't overthink it else you'll regret it later," he cautioned. Siya was miffed but she nodded in acknowledgement.

In an effort to divert the conversation, she said, "Remember I told you that I met my best friend from school at the gallery?" Samar nodded. "Well, Aisha and I met for coffee yesterday..." and she gave him an account of their meetup.

11

Siya had to fight the urge to get on a weighing scale after returning from the gym the next day. Ambika had warned her that she should weigh herself only once a week and that too first thing in the morning.

As Siya ate her breakfast, she mulled over their plans for the upcoming weekend. Samar and she would probably watch a movie if he got home at a reasonable time. At some point, they would take their boys on an outing to a place of their choice. It could be a movie (animation of course) or a gaming arcade (*I hope not—can't stand those noisy places*) or a children's play (*lemme check the schedule at Prithvi)*. Siya would have loved to take them to a garden or a park where they could just run around. Sadly, in Mumbai, options for picnicking in the outdoors were non-existent. They would have to travel out of the city to Lonavala, Khandala or Alibagh. *Food options in these places will definitely not find Ambika's approval…so no picnics. Maybe, we'll just take them for a movie in case we don't watch one ourselves,* Siya decided. And, that's when she remembered that they had been invited to a social event! *Imran and Maya's party is on Saturday.* She was apprehensive at the timing as she wondered how she would stick to her diet. She decided to speak to Ambika and understand the Do's and Don'ts for house parties.

When Samar got home later that night, she reminded him of the dinner invitation. A brief discussion on what to take for their US returned friends followed. Old Monk, which had been Imran's preferred poison back when Samar and he used to hang out, was chosen. Siya was aghast at Samar's suggestion and argued till he explained the emotional connect with Old Monk! Siya then offered to check if their local wine shop had it so Samar could pick it up.

Imran and Samar were childhood friends who had grown up together on the same college campus where their fathers had taught. Imran, who was now a successful psychologist/therapist, had recently moved back to Mumbai after living abroad where he ran a roaring practice for many years. He had decided to come back to India because he missed the warmth of his country. With salt-pepper curly hair, well-manicured hands and an open, honest face, he had a gentle bearing. Siya found him to be rather interesting and handsome and was looking forward to meeting him again.

The ringing of her cell phone disrupted Siya's day dreaming! "Hello! Hi, Siya! It's Aisha. How are you?"

"I'm well, Aisha. What's up?"

"Couple of my friends and I are planning to go shopping to the new R City Mall. Would you like to come along?"

"That sounds like fun! I'd love to. When are you planning to go?"

"We are planning for tomorrow—to get over the mid-week blues! Shopping followed by lunch with girlfriends is prescribed as the best cure, you know," she said, laughing out loud.

"It sure sounds therapeutic, Aisha, but I will come only on one condition."

"Condition? There are no conditions in friendship, my darling!" said Aisha with a dramatic flourish.

Siya giggled. "Don't be *filmy*. It's just that I've started my diet and I'm allowed to eat only what's prescribed so please don't force me."

"Oh! That's a Punjabi thing to do and I'm not one so you are safe!" Aisha answered gleefully. "Hahaha! Also, please don't tell your friends that I'm on a diet. Nobody takes me seriously when I say that, as if my losing weight will be bad for them!"

"Ok. I won't tell…don't worry, ya, just chill. Come along, it'll be fun," said Aisha.

Details decided, plans made, Siya hung up, silently thanking the universe for bringing Aisha back into her life.

12

The next morning, Aisha was supposed to pick Siya up at 11 am. Dressed in khaki coloured linen pants and a white linen shirt from Cotton World, strappy sandals on her feet and her favourite illusion pearl necklace, Siya surveyed her reflection in the elevator mirror. *Not diva like but okay for a day at the mall!*

"Going out?" asked a now familiar voice, as she stepped out of the lift on the ground floor.

Siya stiffened. "Yes," she muttered, avoiding eye contact, hoping to end the conversation there. As she rushed to the porch, she breathed a sigh of relief. *Phew! I'm sure she would not approve of my outfit. Not sexy in the least.*

Just then Aisha arrived to pick her up. As Siya got in beside her, she hugged her warmly. "Siya, meet my friend, Sara," said Aisha, pointing to the front seat where an attractive young woman was seated. Sara turned around and smiled at Siya. "Sara moved from London a couple of months ago. Our kids go to the same school. And, Sara—Siya is my best friend from school. I am so lucky to have found her again!" Aisha said, giving her hand a squeeze. Siya beamed at her and felt reassured.

As Sara, Aisha, and Siya stepped into the cool environs of the glass-fronted mall, a bunch of ladies standing beside the display of a Ritu Kumar store waved out to them. "They are my friends from the building. I hope you are not overwhelmed, Siya," Aisha said, apologetic.

"Not at all, Aisha! It'll be refreshing to meet some new people. I've been so absorbed with my kids and their activities that I haven't really made any friends in the last couple of years."

"Oh, so who do you go shopping and lunching with?" Sara asked with surprise.

Siya looked at her properly—slim fitted blue jeans, sleeveless fuchsia top, fashionable ballerinas, fashion jewellery adorned her ears, neck and wrists. "On my own generally. Occasionally, with my husband," Siya said, simply.

"Oh, you poor thing! What do men know about girls' clothes? My husband hmms and haws if I ask his opinion on clothes or shoes. Takes the joy out of it, if you ask me."

Siya laughed. "That's what my husband does too but I'm so used to shopping by myself that I rarely inflict that pain on him…or myself," she quipped, with a wide smile.

Aisha introduced Siya to all her friends—the sweet, smiling, dimpled Sonia; the sombre and shy Shilpa, and the ethnically attired Jyotika. As they walked from one store to another, Aisha filled her in on the background of her friends, where she had met them, how they had connected and how many kids each one had. The group walked into stores, and tried on different dresses and window-shopped.

Reds, pinks, blues, yellows, and whites—the shops were like an explosion of colours. Siya sighed as she admired the boldly designed and smartly cut dresses. "Go ahead and try one, Siya," whispered Aisha.

"Oh, no, Aisha. I would look like a tent," Siya exclaimed.

"Of course, not. I think this black dress will look really nice on you." Aisha said, holding out a demurely cut, long black dress.

"Nah, this one looks boring."

"Then, try this one." This time she held out a halter-neck black dress with a bare back and little pearls embellishing the loop around the neck. The fabric fell so beautifully, it was perfect.

Siya sighed. "My arms and back will be fully exposed in this...that could scare some people off, you know," Siya laughed nervously.

"Why are you so hard on yourself? Cut yourself some slack," Aisha said as Sara walked out in a peasant style frock that she wanted to buy.

While Sara paid for the dress, Siya browsed through the racks, compiling a wishlist of dresses she would like. *When I've achieved my goal, I'll come back and try that black dress.* Siya promised herself.

Exhausted after marching from store to store for over two hours, the ladies decided to take a break. Sonia suggested a Chinese restaurant on the topmost floor called Dynasty. As they rode the elevator up, Siya was preoccupied with the food options that she could have for lunch. Luckily, she had spoken with Ambika about what she should eat when she was out. "Grills, mostly, or stir-fried food. Salads and clear soups are always a great option. Remember to stay away from cocktails, mocktails, and other sweetened beverages. Fresh lime soda, buttermilk are sensible choices."

On walking into the restaurant, they were informed that there was a buffet spread available for lunch in addition to the menu. "Restaurants are getting smarter. They realise that most people in a mall want to get back to shopping or work. Buffets save everyone so much time and effort," Aisha commented.

After placing their orders for beverages, the ladies made a beeline for the buffet. Siya was thrilled to see there were plenty of stir-fried vegetables and meats to choose from. She served herself, eyeballing the portions so it was not more than 200 grams. "Is that all you are going to eat?" asked Jyotika sceptically, holding a plate piled high with a variety of appetisers and a small bowl of soup.

"No. I'm going to get a bowl of soup too." Siya smiled back, reluctant to be drawn into a conversation over food.

Once they were all seated at the table, the chatter started. Women's lunches are a phenomenon unto themselves. Various topics are talked about with great gusto—from the latest fashion to diet do's and don'ts to parenting issues to handling husbands to murky politics to thought-provoking movies to awe-inspiring celebrities to irritating relatives to sex in all its fifty shades to quirky neighbours to unforgettable books—it can be quite exhilarating when you are with the right mix of people! Siya couldn't recall when she had last had so much fun just chatting with adults! Most of her outings were with Samar and the kids, which was a different kind of fun. *This is so stimulating,* she thought.

The conversation then veered to social media since Sonia's husband worked with Facebook. Siya listened in on the conversation with keen interest and asked many questions. "You don't have a Facebook account, Siya?" Aisha asked, incredulously.

"I do, Aisha. But, I'm not so tech savvy; I haven't explored it much...," she said in a small voice.

"It's a great way to meet like-minded people. You can be a part of so many groups—be it food, fitness, books, theatre, sports… If you are single, you can join a singles' club where you could possibly meet someone interesting," Sonia winked at Jyotika as she championed the concept.

"I enjoy being on Facebook! I have connected with so many people I used to know," added Aisha. "Imagine finding someone you went to school or college with—what fun!" she squealed with delight.

"Wow! I would like to find this boy who lived in my neighbourhood when we were growing up in Baroda. He was bright and funny. I think about him even now. Wonder what he did with his life," Shilpa mused.

"Why don't you search for him, Shilpa?" asked Aisha. "What's holding you back?" she asked in a challenging tone.

Shilpa looked at everyone, a trifle nervous. She was obviously not used to being asked such questions. "I'm a happily married woman, Aisha!" she announced, tight lipped.

"Oh, for God's sake, you're not going to jump into bed with him! Can married women not have male friends? You sound just like my Dad," Aisha muttered, with distaste. "Is that what you're teaching your kids? Not to mingle with the opposite sex?" she added in frustration.

"Of course, not! I don't think like that…I went to a co-ed school, you know. But, why rock the boat?"

Aisha backed off. "Shilpa, it's normal to be curious. I think it's a heart-warming feeling to reconnect with people from your past. As we grow up, life gets complicated. We forget how simple things used to be…and how happy those simple things made us. I'd say—Go for it!" she said, smiling as she squeezed her hand lightly.

"What if I make him uncomfortable?" she asked shyly.

Aisha answered with a twinkle in her eyes. "Then, you wish him a happy life and move on; no harm done."

"The moment people hear that I'm a divorcee, they will want nothing to do with me," Jyotika muttered.

"That's not true, Jo," Sonia answered, giving her a small hug. "Divorce is not a stigma anymore. It's not like in our parents' times—we don't have to stick it out even if we don't get along. It's important to find a person who is mentally compatible with you. After all, you are going to spend your life together," she concluded.

"No two people are alike, Jo. You have to kiss a lot of frogs before you find your Prince," Aisha added. "Sometimes, the frog becomes a Prince. At other times, the Prince transforms into a frog," said Aisha, empathetically. Everyone looked at her, solemnly trying to gauge her intention. Aisha held their gaze.

"I love my frog and he loves me back, thankfully," chipped in Sara, making everyone laugh out loud!

Looking at Aisha sideways, Siya wondered, *the idea of re-connecting with your past is tempting. I could look on Facebook. Aisha could show me…*

Delhi, July 1994

Papa don't preach, I'm in trouble deep—Madonna

I was afraid. I mulled over the facts of my situation as I walked back home. Walking and talking to myself always helped clear my mind. *"It's not advisable to wait anymore, I'm giving you an appointment for 10 am tomorrow. You'll be free to go home by lunch."* Dr Lata had said as she handed me the paper with my case details. At that moment, I realised that she knew. She knew how lonely and scared and helpless I was. She stood to gain the most out of this. *Why shouldn't she? This is her profession. It is how she earns a living. She must have studied many years to become a doctor. How can you expect her to whisper sweet nothings into your ears as her fingers probe you? You have landed yourself in this mess—it is entirely your fault. Why accuse the doctor of being harsh and devoid of sympathy? How sympathetic will your family be when they hear this? They will be angry and devastated. Did you think about that even once when you were exploring sex? But, he should have taken precautions if he wasn't sure. The deal was that we wouldn't go all the way. So much for love. Where is love when I need it the most? What if I don't go to see her tomorrow? Will she be able to track me? Did I leave my home number with her? But, if I don't go then how will I get out of this?*

With these thoughts running through my mind, I didn't realise I had reached home. Thankfully, no one was home just then. I took our spare key from the neighbour's house and heaved a sigh of relief as I entered. Shutting myself in my room, I burst into tears. *Why did this have to happen to me? How stupid of me. What am I going to do? How am I going to do it?* When the tears ebbed, I got up and quickly washed my face before someone walked in. I needed to think. It was time for damage control.

I mulled over my options that afternoon. *Should I call him? No point. He is in another city. There's no way he can come or organise to send money so soon.* Letters and occasional calls (from him) were our modes of communication. I didn't have a number I could call. I needed to let him know but first I had to get this sorted.

Should I just confide in my family? Out of question! They would not understand, they would be worse than Dr Lata. Dad would go ballistic with rage. They didn't approve of girls talking to boys. God knows why they sent me to a co-ed school or college. If they got to know that I had a boyfriend, they would probably keep me under house arrest forever. Dad definitely would…I couldn't even imagine what he would do.

Suicide? No way, too dramatic. I couldn't pull it off. Besides, I didn't want to die, I wanted to live my life! If it could be resolved in other ways then why go to extremes?

Didi? Yes! Why didn't I think of her before? She had access to money. Of course, she was going to be shocked. She would give me a piece of her mind for being stupid and reckless. *I can't avoid that. But, I think she will bail me out. After all, she married for love, much against everyone's wishes. Hopefully, she will empathise.* She was the only person I could reach out to for help. *But, how do I tell her?* "Hi, Didi! How are you? I'm pregnant"? Gosh…putting it in words was going to be difficult. Would she help me? Would she keep it a secret? After many such thoughts, I decided to make the call and find out.

13

Later that night, Siya brought Samar up to date with the exciting events of her day. "I'm so thrilled I've met Aisha again. I got along well with her friends too—very down to earth. Thank God for that!" she exclaimed.

"Hmmm...so, now you don't have to make an effort to be friends with your neighbours," he remarked, despite being engrossed in reading a magazine.

Siya was taken aback at his remark. She hadn't even thought about that. Heaving a sigh of relief, she said, "I didn't think about it that way! Nice of you to point it out. Now, they are all yours. You can charm them with your dimples and chatter!"

Closing his magazine in irritation, Samar looked at her. "Such sarcasm! You're sounding like those women on the TV soaps my mother watches." Siya's face fell. "You can't see anything good in them? They are successful professionally even though they are wives and mothers. You only do a fraction of what they do. I think you could learn a lot from them, if only you'd be open to them." His eyes flashed with anger. Kicking the quilt aside, he got up from the bed and left the room.

Siya was stunned. *I was only teasing. Why did he have to get so upset? And, what does he mean by saying I only do a fraction of what they do? Just because I'm not being paid a salary, I cannot account for every single thing I do. I'm a good homemaker, making sure my kids are well brought up. If I had not given up my career, I would have been a successful professional just like them. But, I made the choice to be with my kids once I decided to have them.*

He sees no value in that… Siya felt an ache deep within. *Am I nothing? Does everything else I do have no value? Then, why am I pushing myself to be a good mother and a good wife all the time? If the only thing that will make him happy is to see me 'work', then I guess I will.*

Samar and Siya were distant with each other the next morning. As Siya got the boys ready for school, she cattily wondered who did the same for Naina and Ira's children. *Stop it, Siya. Focus on what you can do.*

Once the boys were out of the house, Siya got involved with getting Samar's breakfast and lunch ready. Siya would generally sit with him and talk about the day ahead while he ate his breakfast. Although she was sitting beside him, she was lost in her own thoughts. When Samar addressed her by name, she thought it was her mind playing tricks on her until he reached out his hand and touched her arm. "I'm sorry for last night. I didn't mean to say that you do nothing. You take good care of us all." Siya looked at him, her eyes welling with tears. *This is why I love him. He can be hurtful but he sees things in fairness…after his temper has abated.*

"I know," she replied. Blinking the tears away, she said, "What I don't know is what to do with my time."

"Siya, you don't have to go get a job because of me," Samar said, as if reading her mind.

"Samar, I have time on my hands while the kids are away at school. I would love to do something within those hours. The problem is I don't know what."

"Siya, if it makes you feel productive then I'm happy. Don't do anything just to please me or to spite anyone."

"I won't. Now tell me what I enjoyed doing most in the BC era (an acronym Samar and she had created—Before Children)?" He looked at her with a faint smile, gaze fixed on her face. She could hear the tape rewinding in his head.

"Reading," he said, finally.

"Hmmm, I still read…though not as much as I would like to," Siya remarked.

"What about writing?" he asked.

"Oh, that's something I haven't done in a long, long time. Besides, what would I write? And, for whom?"

"People are always looking for content writers."

"Really? Who's going to employ a 30-something woman, mother of two kids, on a sabbatical for almost eight years now to write without any previous experience of the same, Samar?"

"You'll find a way, Siya," Samar answered, giving her a peck on the cheek as he got up, leaving her deep in thought.

14

By Friday, Siya was anxious to see whether her altered food pattern and regular cardio had made a difference. *Dear God, please, please, please let there be some change. Even half a kilo will be good. I just need a sign that I'm on the right track!* Siya prayed as she sat down to her breakfast of one tablespoon oats cooked in milk. She wondered whether she could add a smidgen of honey to make it a tad sweet or whether that would amount to cheating.

The chime of her phone interrupted her thoughts. A new message from Naina!

Hi, Siya! We are having the first get together of our building kitty today. It will be at my place, Flat 201, from 11 am onwards. Hope you can make it.

Oh God… It'll seem really rude if I don't go now that she has sent a personal SMS. Besides, I need to mollify Samar…

Hi, Naina! I'll definitely try to be there. She messaged back.

Now, I must figure out what to wear to the kitty, she grimaced at the thought.

Siya settled on a loose, kalidaar Lucknowi kurta with churidar for the morning. She didn't want to wear anything flashy for the PTM but at the same time, didn't want to appear underdressed for the kitty. As she walked to school, Siya couldn't shake off a sense of anxiety at her chosen attire. As the anxieties mounted, she decided to go home and change before the kitty. By the time she was done at school, it was already 11:30 am. It was noon when she got to Naina's flat—dressed in a navy-blue dress with an

A-line cut. It billowed out from the bust line, camouflaging her belly fat. Strappy silver sandals and silver hoops in her ears completed her look. The door of the flat was opened by Ira.

"Oh, hi!" she said, with a wide smile. "Come on in," she added, appraising her from head to toe.

As Siya walked into the living room, many faces turned towards her and she felt like she was on the sets of *The Bold and the Beautiful*. Lustrous long hair, expensive jewellery, designer clothes, rich perfumes... She smiled at them, recognising some from the annual dinner party.

Naina broke away from a trio of ladies to greet her. "I'm glad you could come. What can I offer you to drink? Tea, coffee, coconut water...or a spritzer?" she asked.

"Er, I'll have some coconut water please." Siya answered.

"Okay. Let me introduce you to some neighbours," she said, handing her a glass of chilled coconut water. Names and flat numbers were exchanged in an effort to know each other better. While some of them were young mothers like her, the rest had older kids in college.

"When is the baby due?" asked a svelte looking woman.

"Sorry?" Siya asked, not sure she had heard her right.

Pointing to her stomach, she asked again, "The baby. When are you due?"

Siya's cheeks flushed. Her ears turned red as she considered how to respond. Just then, Ira jumped into the conversation. "Siya is not pregnant, ladies! In fact, she has just started a diet to lose weight. Right, Siya?" Siya's gaze flitted over the faces waiting for her reply. She didn't know how to respond to such outright cattiness.

"Oh, I'm so sorry. How presumptuous of me," said the svelte woman, placing a hand on her arm.

Seeing the regret in her eyes, Siya gave her a small smile. "It's okay."

"You are absolutely fine, dear. These skinny people think everyone should look like them!" interjected a pleasant faced woman. "But you know, with my deadly beauty, if I also become skinny then who will look at them!" she added with a loud guffaw, making everyone laugh out loud. Siya laughed along, relieved. "Myself Jolly. I live on the fifteenth floor. Come home some time for *gupshup*."

The conversation moved to a woman who was a Home Baker keen to start her own enterprise. Siya enjoyed getting to know the others but she tried to stay away from Ira. Eventually, the conversation veered towards the next social event in the building. As Naina took centrestage to inform everyone that it would be during the Christmas break, chatter erupted. "Why not have something earlier? Christmas is too far away," pointed out one.

"Yes. Let's have a Ganapati or Janmasthami celebration to kickstart the festive season. It'll be nice for the kids to get involved," suggested another.

Naina and Ira exchanged glances. They didn't look very happy at this turn of events. "We'll have to check what our budget allocation is for these events," Naina announced. "I don't know if it's a good idea to celebrate religious festivals. We have some Muslim and Catholic families in our building. They may think of it as unfair," she tried to reason.

"I agree. Besides, so many people celebrate Ganesh Chaturthi and Janmasthami at home. Why not do something that everyone can participate in?" Ira added

"How about a Dandiya night during Navaratri?" Jolly asked, excitedly.

The room erupted in exclamations! Everyone complimented Jolly on her thinking. "That's a great idea, Jolly!" Ira agreed.

"I know an excellent musical group who we can book," Jolly offered, grinning from ear to ear.

"Super! We'll take the details from you," Naina added. Another neighbour offered a catering contact while yet another knew a party organiser who could help with other ideas. Siya couldn't believe how things had worked out. Now, she wouldn't be required to do anything!

As the first group of women decided to leave, Siya joined them, making sure to thank Naina for her hospitality.

Later that night, she gave Samar an update on her day—the PTM, the concerns raised by the teachers and also the kitty party. She was eager to share the discussion on the social events but Samar didn't seem receptive. Although Siya felt dissatisfied at being unable to share, her relief at having received the 'Get out of Jail' card far outweighed her disappointment!

15

After spending the best part of Saturday watching the animation movie *Up* with the boys, Siya was looking forward to spending some time with adults at Imran's place in the evening.

I got a feeling, tonight's gonna be a good night, she hummed, as she draped an indigo and pink Paithani saree. She didn't want to go through the stress of trying out western clothes again. She wanted to feel at ease. Samar looked relaxed in khaki linen pants with a white linen shirt.

"Isn't your saree very formal for a house party?" he asked, eyeing Siya.

"Hmmm… I have very few blouses that fit. This is one of them," she replied in a tone that said *End of discussion,* as they walked out of the house after saying goodnight to the kids.

Imran had bought an apartment in Tivoli, one of the newest buildings in Hiranandani Garden. As Siya and Samar alighted from their car, they marvelled at the well-lit and beautifully laid out garden beyond the porch. With a hundred bulbs in the ceiling of the porch, it gave the impression of being a five-star hotel. As they walked into the lobby, a gentle rippling from the fountain in the centre of the lobby, created a magical hush, making them whisper to each other. A state-of-the-art elevator swiftly whooshed them up to the penthouse, on the thirtieth floor.

They were ushered in by a saree clad, smiling Mausi (the colloquial term used for an elderly female house help in Mumbai) who led them to an aesthetically done up living room. The walls were adorned with pleasing landscapes in gilded frames on one hand while gorgeous Indian antiques, including a nineteenth century *jhoola,* carved exquisitely in sandalwood stood proudly against a wall. Their admiring gaze lighted on Imran and his wife, Maya, who were busy chatting with a young couple, dressed in khadi silk.

"Hey, Samar! Welcome, welcome. What a pleasure to see you again," Imran said, breaking away from the couple to hug them. "Siya, you look enchanting in that saree. You know, I never thought I'd say this but I have really missed the sight of women in sarees. It is, unquestionably, the most graceful attire that adorns a woman."

Siya blushed as she muttered her thanks, shyly. "Here's something for you, Imran, especially selected by your *chaddi buddy,*" she said, as she proffered a red and gold gift bag.

"Sam, since when do you have to bribe me with gifts in exchange for dinner!" Imran exclaimed, pleasantly. As he unwrapped the bottle, the smile vanished from his face. He was stunned into silence. Siya looked at Samar with a worried expression. *Oh oh, have we made a boo-boo?* "Oh my God...this is the best gift ever, man," he announced as he hugged Samar warmly. *"Saaley, tujhe abhi bhi yaad hain?"* he asked.

"Of course! Many an evening was spent drowning our sorrows while we looked for answers from the universe," Samar retorted.

Imran guffawed aloud. "It brings back so many great memories. Maya, come here, look at this," he turned around to call his wife.

Maya excused herself from the couple she had been in conversation with. Imran held the bottle aloft, as if showing off a trophy, a wide smile plastered on his face.

Her eyebrows shot up in surprise. "Aah, I've heard of all the trouble that monk got you guys into!" she said, with a twinkle in her eyes, as she hugged Siya and Samar.

"Siya was apprehensive about this gift. She thought you would enjoy a bottle of Dom Perignon or Beaujolais more."

"Never, Siya! This is just what the psycho needs," Imran declared solemnly, making a dig at himself. "So, what can I offer you, Siya? I know what Samar and me are going to have!" he pointed in the direction of the bar. Siya beamed. *If I ever need a shrink, he would definitely be my first choice!*

"I'll help myself once I'm done admiring the bar," she said as she noticed their Mausi usher in some more guests.

Platters of cheese with plump Californian grapes and crackers, assorted salads with a variety of dressings, trays of tikkas and kebabs were laid out as starters for everyone to help themselves. Just as she was serving herself some salad, Maya appeared by her side. She was a certified yoga instructor who had a flourishing business in the States. Even at the age of forty-two, she had a figure that was the envy of most women. She was five feet eight inches tall and was blessed with a clear complexion. Dark haired and dusky, she didn't look a day over twenty-five despite having two teenaged kids.

Holding the *pallu* of her saree out in admiration, Maya exclaimed, "Siya, I love your saree. It's such a gorgeous Paithani. I have to get myself one of these."

"Thank you! I'd be happy to take you shopping!" Siya answered.

"Oh, that would be fun! Let's do it soon," she said with glee. Siya complimented her on her artistically kept home, remarking at some of the pieces. "So, what do you enjoy doing besides shopping?" she asked.

Siya was taken aback. Nobody had ever asked her that. If she was meeting someone for the first time, they would try to ascertain which organisation she worked in. Upon discovering that she didn't have a career, most people just lost interest or moved on to general topics. Nobody asked her what she enjoyed doing. Hell, she was not sure if she knew herself!

"I used to enjoy reading, writing and music a lot. Of late, I've been so consumed with the kids that I don't seem to have the time or energy for anything else. I love doing things with them, for them...although I do miss getting ready every day and going off to work sometimes," she stopped, suddenly self-conscious that she'd shared too much.

Maya nodded in response. "I hear you, Siya. We women take a backseat when it comes to our own selves. But, it's very important to make the time to do what you enjoy," Maya said, earnestly.

"I volunteered to teach and help out with kids at an NGO for a while but my heart was not it. I felt bad that I couldn't be selfless and giving like other volunteers there," Siya continued pouring her heart out in a small voice.

Maya said to her, warmly, "Don't be hard on yourself, Siya. It takes a while to figure things out. You are young, your journey has just started."

"Maya, I'm sorry for off-loading on you like this. I don't generally do this," she apologised.

"Don't be silly. I'm glad you're talking to me. You know, when you articulate your thoughts and feelings, it brings clarity. You're able to deal with it better." She smiled in encouragement. Siya nodded in relief.

"What else is going on in your life?" she persisted.

Siya couldn't help saying, "I'm on a diet, I want to lose 15 kgs." Siya hadn't told anyone about her diet yet; she was waiting for the scales to show some change before she shared it. Maya made her feel at ease so she could share freely. The conversation moved to the details of her diet and Maya even offered to help Siya with yoga. They made plans of catching up for a cup of coffee, before Maya got called away by other guests.

As the evening advanced, everyone veered towards the balcony of Imran's penthouse. Conversation flowed freely as alcohol made everyone at ease. When one of the guests asked Imran how he had met Maya, all eyes turned towards him! "A good psychologist does not talk. He plies his guests with food and wine so they feel comfortable enough to talk!" said Imran, oozing charm.

"But we also want to know how brilliant psychologists woo their women. Do they really know what women want?" Samar insisted.

Imran gave him a mischievous smile as his eyes rested on his wife, Maya. "We met in my office actually. She was a patient at first. After she finished her sessions, we lost touch. I met her a couple of months later at her yoga studio. Call it a coincidence. We picked up where we had left off...so, you see—I did know what 'this' woman wanted."

"Unfair advantage," protested Samar in a good-humoured tone.

"Neel, what about you?" someone asked a stylishly dressed, bespectacled man who stood quietly in a corner, nursing a drink. "Where is *bhabhiji*?"

"She's at home...she wasn't feeling too well," he muttered.

"Never mind…you can share with us how you two got married," Sanjay persisted.

"Ours was an arranged love marriage actually. I'd fallen for her at first sight. Bugged my parents to send a proposal when I got transferred to the US. Thankfully, they agreed!" his voice trailed off.

"Neel and I know each other from the US," added Imran. "He's an investment banker. He used to work with Lehmann Brothers. Fortunately, he moved in good time." Everyone nodded in empathy, knowing how that company had gone bankrupt to everyone's shock. "He works with JP Morgan now. Coincidentally, we moved around the same time to the same township in Mumbai," Imran added, smiling at Neel.

What a narrow escape! Lucky guy. Wait a minute, why does his story sound familiar? Have I heard this before? Siya wondered, unable to place it.

Returning home around 2 am, Siya pondered over the wonderful time they'd had. Samar and she discussed the highlights of their evening as they changed and drifted off to sleep.

16

The next morning, Samar woke up with a start. He was jolted out of his sleep at the sound of Siya's scream. He sprung out of bed and made his way to the bathroom. Siya was standing on the weighing scale, beaming like a kid on Christmas morning! "I've lost one kilo, Samar! I've lost one kilo! I can't believe it... I'm so happy and relieved," she said as she hugged him tightly. "I really didn't think it was possible. I was full of doubt."

"That's great, Siya!" he said, hugging her back. "Wait a minute, does this mean we will all have to eat salads for a long time to come?" he teased.

Siya called Ambika right away to share the news with her but there was no reply on her phone. She messaged her soon after: *I've lost it, Ambika! I've lost one kilo in one week! Yay!*

"So, should we celebrate this momentous occasion?" Samar asked, as she put her phone away.

"Celebrate? No way! I have to lose another fourteen kilos before I do that, Samar. I'm going to have to put more thought and effort into my diet. I will have to increase my cardio too," she elaborated in earnest.

"Okay, okay! We'll hold off a full-blown celebration for now," he answered.

Aryan and Arjun had overheard their conversation and latched on to the word 'celebration'! Samar and Siya decided to take them out for breakfast at Aromas. "But first, Mama and Papa will go for a walk to Heritage Park while you kids splash around in the pool," Samar suggested. The plan was received with high fives all the way!

As Siya was getting ready to leave, her phone buzzed. It was a message from Aisha.

Hi! What are you doing today? Free to meet for coffee some time?

S: Had a late night yesterday. Just want to relax today. Why don't you and your husband come over for tea in the evening?

A: *He is travelling. Can we meet at a café outside?*

Siya was puzzled. *Why doesn't she want to come home?*

S: Can't confirm just yet. Taking the kids to the pool followed by breakfast. Can I message you later?

A: *OK.*

S: *Is everything okay?*

A: *Yes.*

The Forest Club was situated at the heart of the township, adjacent to a mini forest, making it accessible to residents of all buildings. Other than the swimming pool, it also housed a Squash court, a state-of-the-art indoor badminton court, a gym, sauna and steam rooms in addition to halls where group fitness classes were held. Tennis courts were located behind the clubhouse. Like everything else in Hiranandani, it was a place where people converged. They dropped the kids off at the Forest Club half an hour later, as Siya belted a whole list of instructions to the boys and Vaishali.

Driving past the tall towers that flanked the road, Siya and Samar marvelled at how lucky they were to be living in a complex that had so many open spaces and facilities, unlike the more crowded (albeit hip) parts of Mumbai.

"Let's stretch before we start walking," Siya told Samar as they entered the Heritage Park. The walking track looped around a beautifully kept garden that was landscaped with boulders, fountains, and a variety of flowering trees and shrubs. Walking beside Samar was always challenging for Siya. At six feet, he effortlessly took big steps as Siya huffed and puffed, trying to catch up with him.

"It's so pleasant here in the mornings. We should come here more often. I'm sure the boys will enjoy running around too," said Siya, taking in the various groups of people spread all over. The crowd consisted mostly of elderly people and young families, dressed in relaxed sportswear.

Up ahead in the distance, Siya spotted a lissome lady in a racer back tee, jogging. *She looks familiar. Could it be Aisha?* "Samar, I think that's my friend, Aisha. Remember I told you about her? She messaged me this morning about meeting up but I declined."

"Why? You don't want to meet her?" he asked.

"It's not that. We'd planned our day with the kids. I asked her to come over for tea but she insisted on meeting at a café…her husband is travelling."

"Doesn't she have kids too?"

"Yes, she does. Two boys, just like us."

"I don't think we can catch up with her speed. Let's just wait for her to pass by…"

"Aisha!" Siya called out aloud as she whooshed by them a few minutes later. She didn't stop, focussed on running.

"Must be the earphones," Samar explained.

Siya nodded, keeping her eye on Aisha as she ran the loop. She reached out and touched her arm as she passed by them again. Aisha was startled. "Oh! Hi, Siya! I didn't expect to see you here," she said, pulling out her earphones, resisting Siya's hug. "Don't want to get you drenched in my sweat," she offered, by way of explanation.

Siya nodded in assent. "Aisha, meet Samar. You met him at our wedding but that was years ago," Siya laughed. As Aisha shook hands with Samar, Siya said, "Hey, I'm sorry I won't be able to make it for coffee today. Kids have their own plans lined up."

"No problem, Siya. I understand." Aisha said, giving her arm a reassuring pat.

"Aisha, I've lost one kilo! Can you believe it? I'm so happy!" announced Siya.

"That's great, Siya. You'll manage to lose the rest too." Siya beamed at the vote of confidence.

"Your husband isn't here?" Siya asked.

"I told you he's travelling. Took a morning flight..."

"What does he do?" Samar asked, politely.

"He is an investment banker," she answered.

"Lucrative profession to be in," he remarked.

"Yeah. Very demanding too. He has been inundated with work ever since we got here," Aisha added, dryly.

"Siya, why don't you call them over?" Samar turned to ask Siya.

"It's been on my mind, Samar, but I've been so consumed with this diet that I can't think of anything else!" Siya looked apologetically at Aisha.

"Don't be silly! No formalities with me. In fact, we should have you guys over once my husband is in town for a reasonably long stretch of time. Let me not hold you from your walk anymore," she said, air kissing Siya and waving bye to Samar.

"She seems like a nice person," said Samar as soon as Aisha was out of earshot.

Ambika's reply came late that evening:

That's great, Siya. Will send your 2nd diet plan by email today. Please call me if you have any questions. All the best.

The next morning, Siya messaged Aisha and asked her if she wanted to meet up for coffee.

Aisha refused saying she was occupied with something and that she would get back in touch.

Siya wondered whether her refusal to meet her yesterday had put Aisha off and decided that she would call her soon.

Over the next few weeks, propelled by guilt, Siya tried to call Aisha a couple of times. At times, Aisha would message her saying she was travelling and would call back. Occasionally, Aisha would answer the phone and say she was busy and would call her back later. She didn't.

Eventually, Siya stopped trying. *There is a limit to how much effort I can make. If she cares enough, she'll get in touch. If not...*that was something Siya didn't want to dwell on.

17

"Hi! I'm sorry I've been incommunicado for so long! Lots of family get togethers came up suddenly. Had to travel to Delhi. Are you free to meet some time?"

Siya read Aisha's message as she stepped out of the bathroom. *Finally, she messages after three weeks,* she smiled to herself.

"Silly girl. I'll make time to meet you. Just say when," she replied

"Tomorrow, 11 am at Aromas? PS: I love you!" came the reply almost instantly!

The next morning, as Siya dressed up for her coffee date with Aisha, she was in for a pleasant surprise! *Oh my God, these trousers are actually loose on me now! I think I'll need a belt to keep it up. Yippee!* Siya broke into a jig then and there. It was finally happening for her. She was overjoyed! The floral top she had decided to wear also hung comfortably loose on her frame. Siya couldn't stop beaming!

Knowing that she was losing weight the right way had put a spring in her step. She was humming Gloria Gaynor's 'I will survive' as she stepped out of her apartment. "Someone's chirpy today," said a familiar voice. Siya turned around as Naina was stepping out of Ira's flat.

"Hi, Naina! How are you?" she said, beaming at her dressed in workout clothes with beads of perspiration on her forehead, as she entered the elevator.

"I'm so tired. Just finished a rigorous kickboxing workout. I just want to shower and relax," she sighed. "Oh, I'm glad I bumped into you. Remember we were talking about celebrating Navaratri? We've got a go ahead for the budget so we were thinking of putting together a sequence of popular songs from Hindi movies over the years. Based on how many people turn up for practice sessions, we can decide the number of songs. We will organise the first session over a weekend so that even working people can join in." Just then, the elevator doors opened on to Naina's floor. "I'll see you at the practice session. Date and time will be shared through a circular. Bye," she said as she walked out. Siya gaped at her back, unsure if she should join in. She disliked being taken for granted.

"Hey, you've lost weight since our last meeting," said Aisha, hugging Siya as she walked into Aromas.

"I have. Five kilos!" declared Siya, with a mix of delight, pride, and gratitude.

"Wow! That's fantastic! I'm so happy for you," Aisha beamed.

"I still have a long way to go...before I can look stunning like you," said Siya, eyeing her toned arms and shoulders in the simple spaghetti strapped top she wore. "For starters, you'll have to start showing more skin!" Aisha said, sticking her tongue out at Siya. "Jokes apart, you carry yourself so gracefully that you will look naturally stunning once you achieve your weight loss goal."

"I love you, Aisha! You know exactly what I need to hear and when I need to hear it..."

"Why? What happened?" Aisha asked, with concern.

"It's these divas in my building..." And Siya filled her in.

"Not cool!" Aisha grimaced, as Siya narrated how Ira made gibes at her, making her feel inadequate and unattractive. "To top it all, I don't have a job or a vocation of any other sort...so they assume that I'll participate in every event they organise even if I'm not cut out for it. Sometimes, I feel they just want to have a good laugh at my expense!"

"Phew. That's a lot of emotional download for one morning! Let's take it one by one. What do you want to do, Siya? I mean, work wise. What will bring you satisfaction?" Aisha asked.

"Writing!" Siya answered in a heartbeat.

"Okay. What kind of writing? Fiction/non-fiction? Technical? Financial? Sports?"

"Sports! Yeah, right—do I look like someone who enjoys sports, Aisha?"

"Oh, shut up! Don't be so whiny...a lot of sports fans are fat!" she said, digging her fingers into Siya's belly. Aisha encouraged her and probed again as to what kind of writing she would enjoy.

As Siya thought over it, Aisha fished her cell phone out of her handbag and browsed her contacts list. She decided to introduce her to Manoj Nayak, an acquaintance who was launching a community networking site for Powai and was looking for writers to cover various aspects of life in the township. She decided she would host a party (which was overdue) and invite them all. Siya was touched at the effort she was willing to make on her behalf.

Aisha also advised her to surround herself with positive people, people who looked beyond physical appearances. Siya looked at her earnestly as her mind browsed the images of people she met regularly—at school, in the gym, at the salon, in the building. "Re-connecting with people in your past can be a great morale booster, you know." Aisha continued, with a secretive smile. "You are on Facebook, right?" Siya nodded. "Well then, use it to your advantage. Those people who know you for who you were back then will be happy to reconnect with you even now. Nostalgia is a great adhesive for relationships. Who knows what opportunites can come your way !" she said as she snapped her fingers.

Siya was awestruck. "How did you get to be so smart and wise?" she asked, with a twinkle in her eyes.

"Because I'm curious. I explore. I'm not happy being comfortable. Life is too fleeting, so live every day to the fullest!" she said as she rose up and reached out to hug her. "Gotta go! Will message you details of dinner after checking Neel's schedule. Bye," and she rushed out as Siya sat, looking at her walking away. *She looks really happy today… good for her. I'm glad she called me back; I've missed her.*

Walking back home from Aromas, Siya marvelled at how patiently Aisha had listened to her rant. She was not accustomed to talking about things with anyone other than Samar… *And, how easily she provided credible solutions. Just what I need! I wonder if it's worth exploring…reconnecting with people from my past. What harm could come out of it? I can always unfriend or block a person I don't want to chat with.*

18

She logged into Facebook when she got home and following Aisha's advice, searched for some names from her past. With some trepidation, she typed in the name she was looking for—SIDDHANT MALHOTRA. She clicked enter and waited, a trifle nervous. How would it feel seeing his face again, after so many years? A plethora of images appeared on her screen immediately. She scanned the faces one by one but could not spot him. She then decided to look for his friends instead, those whose names she remembered.

Sumit Kapoor, Ashish Seth, Bindu Lal, Nivedita Thakur, Sameer Khanna, Rahul Sood...she found some. Just looking at their faces again was surreal. They were all a part of that time in her life which had passed long ago. She was transported back in time to all the fun they had in college, the bonds they had formed, their unending chat sessions and outings. Amongst them all, Siddhant had been the one for her. They shared a lot of common interests—books, theatre, and music being foremost. In those days, they didn't have the money or the permission of their parents to go out late at night. So, they made the most of the hours they could spend together.

Keen to find his profile, she continued her search. She mulled over some combinations and tried to search with school name, college name, hometown...but to no avail. Finally, it struck her—Shankar! *Yes, that's the surname he preferred to use.* She typed Siddhant Shankar into the search bar and waited. A new page loaded on her laptop with his name. His face was looking at her with an open, hearty smile. Siya froze. *Oh my God, it's him. For real.* As she stared at his face in disbelief, tears welled up till she could see no more...she closed her eyes and they rolled down.

Siya's head churned with myriad thoughts as she ate her lunch in silence. She couldn't even taste it. As she plodded through her stir fry, she planned what to do next. She wondered if she should send him a friend request. She was worried he may decline, or worse, accept it and start stalking her. She even wondered if she should send him a private message, which would be more discreet. After much to-and-fro, she finally sent him a friendly message:

Hi! Remember me? I was just browsing Facebook and your name popped up in a list of 'People you may know'. How have you been?

After sending it, Siya wondered whether she should tell Samar. She didn't like to keep things from him. She knew of some women who did. Even guilty indulgences like a new outfit or a piece of jewellery weren't shared. A writer friend had once shared that a lady told her husband over the phone that she was volunteering at an NGO when she was actually sitting in the parlour next to her! Siya could never do that. Her conscience would never let her. She had realised early in life that it pays to silence your conscience by speaking the truth, however uncomfortable it may be. If she didn't say what was on her mind then it tended to come out, uncalled for, at the most inopportune moments; making her look more foolish or bitchy depending on the situation. She decided she would tell Samar only if she exchanged more than a couple of messages with Siddhant. If the response was just a polite one, it didn't warrant sharing, she mused.

Samar noticed that Siya was lost in thought at dinner that night. He wanted to know if her diet plan was bothering her. Siya assured him that she was enjoying her diet and was actually considering changing everyone's eating habits at home. Her response was met with much opposition from Samar and the boys!

Siya logged into her Facebook account after dinner when she was sure that Samar was totally engrossed in a game on his laptop. She checked her Message box—nothing there. She felt like a teenager as she fretted anxiously. *Has he not replied deliberately or because he has not seen it yet?*

Delhi, July 1994

Girls just wanna have fun—Cyndi Lauper

I looked around to make sure no one I knew was watching me. With trepidation, I climbed the steps leading up to the nursing home. A dark passage led to the reception where the lady receptionist looked up at me briefly and continued to write something. I waited for her to finish, using the time to form the words in my head. She sensed my eyes on her after a while. She looked at me questioningly, with a bored expression.

"I want to see Dr Lata," I said.

"*Wait karo. Woh busy hain,*" she said, dispassionately, without making eye contact.

"How long will it take?" I asked, nervously.

"I don't know, madam. *Patient ke saath hain. Kya kaam hain aapko?"*

"She knows," I remember thinking. I became uneasy. *"Main wait kartee hoon,"* I said.

As I waited, I picked up an old film magazine that was lying on the centre table. Its cover was folding at the corners, as if it was rolled into a fan frequently. It was only then I realised that the reception had no ceiling fan. A solitary pedestal fan, oscillating from side to side, was perched on top of a side-board. *What kind of doctor would let her staff suffer with a fan in the Delhi summer*? I thought. *The really stingy kind,* my second track answered. *No wonder the receptionist is so grumpy.*

I started flipping through the magazine hoping that it would distract me. I came upon the Agony Aunt column. People writing to complete strangers about their private, personal problems for solutions. I scanned a few quickly. They were about extramarital affairs, lovers torn apart, teenage love stories. *Love sure makes the world go round,* I thought, thinking about how I'd fallen in love with the boy who spoke in English.

He had reached out to me to apologise for making that call soon after. It started as a casual friendship but soon we met every day. We explored the city together, driving around on a borrowed motorbike, revelling in our freedom. Movies, plays, music concerts—those that were free. We also explored each other, spending nights together on the pretext of some college festival or the other. I was upset when I found out soon after that he had chosen to pursue his desire to join the army. He had to move to another city. Soon. Our last meeting was passion ridden…as if we were trying to cram in months of loving into one night.

"Madam. Oye, madam..." the receptionist's shrill voice pierced through my happy flashback. Looking at me with irritation, she muttered, "Since when I've been calling you. Doctor is a busy lady. She can't wait for you to finish dreaming."

"I'm sorry," I said, feeling embarrassed. I quickly placed the magazine back on the table and stood up. My first instinct was to run away. I was not ready for this. I stood there, debating with myself.

"Madam, hurry up. Doctor is busy," the receptionist almost shouted as I stood wringing my hands, vacillating.

I sent a little prayer heavenward as I walked towards the doctor's room, my heart thumping.

Dr Lata looked at me through her cat-eye framed glasses, as I walked through the door. I could feel her eyes piercing through my mind, trying to ascertain my problem. Sitting in a high-backed chair, she towered over me, being a big built woman. Or, maybe, I was feeling really small. With spectacles that made her look stern and an unsmiling expression, she didn't make me feel any more comfortable than the receptionist. She opened the dialogue in a business-like manner, wasting no time on pleasantries. She asked me basic questions at first—name, age, frequency of menstrual cycle, weight etc. I had never been to a doctor by myself, without an elder or my sister in tow. They generally handled those questions. I felt a little squeamish when she asked about my periods but I managed to answer her with a straight face.

Then, she asked me what the problem was. Why had I come to see her. I froze for a second. *Should I?* I wondered. *I'd rather not*, I decided. "My periods have been really delayed this time." I muttered, as I clasped my hands together. As if on cue, she asked me if I was sexually active. I gaped at her, not knowing what to say. Was she going to judge me? What if she gave me a lecture on what happens to girls who are 'fast'?

"Do you have a boyfriend?" she asked. I nodded, hesitantly. "Have you had sexual intercourse with him?" she continued. *Gosh! It sounds so devoid of emotion when you put it like that,* the die-hard romantic in me thought.

I sat there wondering how I should answer that question. She didn't try to make it easy for me. "Yes, we did recently," I answered, finally.

"Hmmm" she grunted. "I will need to do a physical examination. Lie down there," she instructed, pointing to the bed against the wall. I got up from the chair and lay on the bed. She put on her rubber gloves and approached me. She unbuttoned my jeans and I stiffened. She asked me to pull it down along with my panty and parted my legs as her gloved fingers started probing my vagina. I gasped. It was sudden and brusque. I winced in pain and discomfort as her fingers kept digging deeper into me. It was so humiliating. Ironically, I felt violated and scared. I blinked back the tears furiously before she could see them. A few minutes later, she pulled out her fingers and asked me to get dressed. My cheeks were hot with embarrassment. I got up and faced the wall as I got dressed, not sure I had come to the right place.

"You are pregnant. The foetus is six weeks old," she announced, as I took a seat gingerly. *Oh fuck. Oh no. Oh God, what am I going to do*? I just stared at her, lips pursed, keeping myself from breaking down.

"Do your parents know?" she asked. I nodded in the negative, not trusting myself to speak without bawling.

"What about your boyfriend?" she asked. I inhaled as I shut my eyes to stop myself from crying.

"He doesn't live here. He's a cadet in the Defence Academy in Pune," I answered, in a reasonably calm voice. As I uttered those words, it struck me just how far away he was. And how alone I was. And the deep shit I was in.

"You need to have an abortion at the earliest. It could be dangerous if you postpone it," she declared, solemnly. So many questions erupted in my mind—about the procedure, the duration, the cost. I voiced them as coherently as I could. Without going into details, she said, "It will take a couple of hours after which you can go home. You need to bring an adult along to sign a declaration form absolving the clinic of any responsibility in case something goes wrong." *Oh my God! Wrong…what could go wrong? Who could I bring along? Nobody knew that my boyfriend and I were so…intimate. I could take a day off from work and come alone. But, what if something happened to me? What if I died? It happened all the time in movies. I can't die. I don't want to die. I've only just graduated and started working. I want to do so much more. He has to become an officer and then we can be together*. There was no point sharing my anxieties a stranger who wouldn't empathise.

"How much will it cost?" I asked, bracing myself.

"It will cost Rs 10,000," she said, matter-of-factly.

OH MY GOD… My mind went numb. Where the fuck was I going to get that much money? My salary was only Rs 6,000 and I hadn't even completed one month yet. *I'm sure they won't give me an advance so soon. Who can I borrow so much money from? I AM SCREWED.*

19

N*eel is in town this Friday. Dinner at our place is on. I hope Samar and you are free to join in.*

A message from Aisha flashed on her cell phone as she checked it after her workout the next morning.

S: *Yes, we are! Looking forward to meeting your husband. Who else will be there?*

Almost immediately, she got a reply:

Some neighbours and hopefully, Manoj from Powai Info.

Siya had spent most of the previous day waiting for a response on Facebook. She was tempted to log into her Facebook account after she got home but decided not to. Instead, she went through the motions of the day—planning menus, shopping for groceries and the drill.

When she was walking down an aisle at the local supermarket, she heard a familiar voice call out to her. It was Paru, dressed in blue and green from head to toe! Siya greeted her warmly as Paru remarked, "You're looking slim, Siya! The diet plan seems to be working!"

"Yes, it is! I've lost five kilos. I love the colours you're wearing—one of my favourite combinations!" said Siya, returning the compliment.

"Has it been difficult?"

"I'll be lying if I say no. The first one or two kilos were tough but now, I've got into the rhythm."

"I know what you mean. Initially, you have to condition your mind to believe that this much food is sufficient. Then, you realise that it's actually more than enough. And, once you see results, then it boosts your confidence. The brain sends positive signals and before you know it, you've achieved your goal!" declared Paru.

"Haha! You make it sound so ridiculously easy!"

"You can do it, Siya. If you have stuck with it this long then I'm sure you will achieve it." Paru encouraged her and then left hurriedly to complete her chores.

As Siya watched Paru push her trolley towards the payment counter, she thought that she should spend more time with her. *Paru is such a cheerful, positive person.* She went through the motions of grocery shopping disinterestedly, fully aware that all she wanted to do was check her laptop. She got home and impatiently ran to the bedroom, on the pretext of running to the loo!

She grabbed the laptop and logged into Facebook. She waited as the page loaded. *No message notification. Hmmm... how long does it take to reply? Stop it, Siya. Get a grip on yourself.* She was cheesed off now. At herself. And, him.

It was in the afternoon after the boys returned that a new notification popped up on Facebook. They were sitting around the dining table, Siya having her tea and the boys tucking into their snack. Siddhant had finally replied!

Of course, I remember you, Siya! How can I ever forget? It's been so long since I last saw you. You look good. I'm currently posted in a remote location. It takes a while to access the internet. Let me send you a friend request. Oh, my cell number is 8130552322. What's yours?

She felt good reading his response but was not sure about sharing her number. Aryan's voice brought her to the present and she got busy attending to him.

She then read his message over and over again and framed an adequate response to his reply.

She didn't want to sound excited. She was trying to achieve a tone of cordiality—not too hot, not too cold. After much thinking, she came up with a response and sent it, even as she analysed her own reply. *You're flirting a bit in the first lines... No, I'm not! Okay, maybe a little bit. But, it's Sid...that's how I was with him.*

20

On Friday, Siya reminded Samar that they had a dinner invitation at Aisha's, as he was getting dressed for work. Samar had forgotten but he quickly informed her that he should be back by 7:30 pm.

After returning from the gym, Siya showered quickly because she had decided to check which clothes fit her. Moving the front pile of clothes in the almirah to one side, she reached into the back where she had relegated her party wear. A dozen clothes spilled all over as she tried to drag the pile ahead. Picking them up from the floor, she placed them on the bed. An explosion of colours—fuchsia, turquoise, canary yellow, black, crimson red, emerald green—made the pile look like a painted canvas against the off-white sheet on her bed.

Gingerly, she picked up the clothes one by one, enjoying the feel of different textures on her fingertips. She gasped at how beautifully the clothes were designed. Some of them had been picked up by Samar on his travels abroad—they were distinctly different in their cuts and palette of colours. Some had been bought by her, fifteen kilos ago, in the BC era! *Hmmm...at least we have good taste,* she thought, holding an off white, sequined top in front of her. It was the same top she had tried to put on, a few weeks ago, with no success. Her cheeks reddened as she recalled how frustrated she had felt then. She opened the button at the neck and turned it around. *Please, please fit,* she muttered under her breath as she held it above her head. Inserting her arms into the arm holes one by one, she pulled it down over her torso.

It slid like a waterfall! She looked at her reflection in the mirror. *It fit!*

Aisha lived in one of the newer buildings of Hiranandani called Octavius. Alighting from their car, Samar and Siya took in the newness of the marble lobby and the green open spaces. "Looks fancy," Samar commented. The elevator whizzed them to the fifteenth floor soundlessly.

"What a contrast to our groaning, antiquated lift," exclaimed Siya. The door was opened almost immediately after they rung the bell by Aisha, who looked stunning in a black halter neck top and cigarette pants; sans jewellery.

"Siya! I'm so glad you're the early birds. It'll give us some time alone before the others join in," Aisha said, as she hugged her warmly. Holding her hand, she pulled her inside. "You look fabulous in this top, Siya! Been shopping, I see!"

"No way, it's too early for that. This is something I dug up from a pile marked 'Perish the thought' in my almirah."

"Haha! You're funny. But, so hard on yourself. Isn't she, Samar?" she said to him with a shy smile.

"That she is, but then I guess that drives her."

Walking down the corridor into the house, Siya could see a lot of steel and chrome furniture, tastefully upholstered in different coloured leather. Photographs, not paintings, hung on the walls. Some were in colour, like the sunrise over the Golden Gate bridge, while others were black and white, capturing the essence of various bustling metros all over the world. An entire wall was adorned with pictures of the family—kids, uncles, aunts, grandparents. While Siya recognised her Naani and siblings, Aisha had to point out her kids and Neel's family. Splashes of colour in the form of candle stands and fresh flowers brought some relief to the minimalist décor of the house. "Neel, this is Siya!" she announced to the crouching back of her husband, who was trying to connect his Bose system to some fancy gadget she didn't recognise.

Turning around, he beamed at them as he stood up. "What a pleasure to finally meet you, Siya. Aisha cannot stop talking about you!" he said, giving her hand a gentle squeeze.

Siya looked wide eyed. "Haven't we met before?" she asked.

Neel's eyes narrowed as he looked from Siya to Samar and back. "Have we?" he asked, unable to place them.

"Yes. At Imran's party! Weren't you there?" Siya replied.

Samar chimed in, "Oh, yes...we did meet there. You were alone."

Neel's cheeks reddened as his eyes met Aisha's. "Of course, I remember now," he said smoothly, "I had no idea you were Aisha's friend! Else, I would have spent the evening extracting her secrets from you!" he added with a laugh.

"One evening won't be enough for that, Neel," Aisha remarked, her eyes sparkling with challenge. "While we are on the subject, I must tell you, Samar, that I have a stash of information on Siya!" she continued.

"Really? I would pay anything to hear her stories! She doesn't talk much about her school or college days," he said, putting his arm around her shoulder.

"Great! Let me get you a drink so we can get started then," Neel offered, trooping off to the bar.

A black leather-clad bar unit on a steel frame stood in one corner of the dining area. While Samar was busy chatting with Aisha, Siya observed Neel. He was of medium height, maybe five eight or five nine, bespectacled and wheatish in complexion. He was dressed in well-fitted blue designer jeans and an olive-green Ralph Lauren polo t-shirt. Designer moccasin shoes in brown suede and Hilfiger framed spectacles complemented the aura of prosperity and sophistication that he exuded effortlessly. *They are definitely doing very well. Expensive taste in home décor, very magazine like. There's something amiss... He looks like a regular guy, but for his expensive taste. Aisha is too stunning for him. He must be super intelligent, I'm guessing!*

Her reverie was broken when Aisha tapped her gently on the shoulder as Neel held out a glass of white wine. "Wine? For me?" she asked.

"Of course! We are celebrating our friendship, Siya. You can't say no," announced Aisha.

Siya took the glass and smiled at the faces watching her. Raising her glass and clinking it with Aisha's, she announced, "To old friends and new!" The toast was repeated as more glasses clinked together.

As the evening progressed, they were joined by the Banerjees and the Shahs, two couples who Neel knew from work and two other couples who lived in the same building. Manoj was the only one who had come by himself. He was in his mid-thirties, of medium height and divorced. He not only wore spectacles but also a sombre expression most of the time. He walked in measured steps and rarely smiled. "That's the gentleman from *Powai Info* who I was talking about. He's looking for freelance writers. Let me introduce you two," Aisha said, interrupting Siya who was in conversation with her neighbours.

Siya excused herself and turned around to face Aisha. "What am I going to tell him? That I used to be on the editorial board of my college magazine? That's not enough to get me a job!"

"Who said anything about a job? It's an opportunity to dust off the cobwebs from a skill that has not been used. Don't undermine yourself."

She dragged her across the living room to where the men were chatting, next to the balcony. Giving him a gentle tap on his shoulder, she said, "Manoj, I'd like you to meet a dear friend of mine, Siya. Remember you'd said you are looking for freelance writers? Well, Siya used to write in school and college. She's been looking for an opportunity to start again. You should get her to write for you, she's really good!" said Aisha with a flourish, leaving them to carry on conversing.

Siya smiled apologetically at Manoj. "Aisha is very keen that I start writing again. She told me about this project that you want to launch," her voice trailed off.

Manoj smiled shyly. "Yes. It's a social networking website aimed at bringing the community together online to discuss and debate issues that affect the quality of their lives in Powai. It will also provide a platform for people to search, advise, recommend and share information on varied topics like the best gyms in the area, good restaurants, banquet halls, doctor referrals, hiring domestic staff etc."

Siya could envision the potential good that could come out of it. "I make money out of the ads people place on my site. If you have a look at it, you will know that it's not much as of now. However, if you can help with selling ad space, then that would enable me to pay you more as a writer. Do you think you can do it?"

"I'm afraid selling is not one of my strengths. I can write... I'd be happy to cover any local events or issues for you but I'm not cut out for sales," she said, wondering if she had just sabotaged an opportunity.

"I understand. It'll help if you talk about us to people you meet. Can you share some of your written pieces? Do you have a blog?"

"No, I'm afraid I don't. But, if you give me something to write about, I could send you a draft to read. If you like it then we can talk."

"That sounds reasonable. For starters, why don't you write about something that's close to your heart."

"Hmmm...like what?" Siya asked.

"Kids! Do you have kids?"

"Yes, I have two boys."

"Great! Then you can write about the open spaces for kids to play in Hiranandani or the various activities available here. These are just some ideas off the top of my head. You could write about anything related to them. I have found that one of the surest ways to get people involved in a community is to talk about issues focusing on kids."

"You're right there! Great. I will send you a piece by email then."

Taking his wallet out from his back pocket, Manoj handed her a business card with his contact details. As Siya was thanking him, they were joined by Neel. "Looks like some deals are being made."

"Haha! No wonder the investment banker has found his way here!" quipped Manoj with a hearty laugh.

"Let me refill my drink before the interrogation begins," chimed Manoj, with a twinkle in his eyes, promising to rejoin them.

Siya turned to Neel and smiled. "I didn't know he had a sense of humour. He looked so serious and sombre to me."

"Oh, Manoj is a good guy. He's just been through a messy divorce. It can really pull you down."

"Hmmm, I didn't know that. It must be tough."

"Yeah…listen, I know I've already said this before but I am really thankful that Aisha has reconnected with you. She used to have mood swings for a long time. In fact, she went into depression a while back. Had to take sleeping pills too. That's one of the reasons we moved back. I couldn't bear to see her like that," Neel turned around away from her, towards the balcony overlooking the lake, as he said that.

Siya was taken aback. *Aisha was depressed? That's hard to believe…she is so full of life.* Siya watched Neel's back. *Was he crying? Oh my God…* She wasn't sure if it would be appropriate to comfort him with a hug. Instead, she reached out and touched his shoulder gently.

"You did the right thing, Neel. Aisha is happy here."

Turning around to face her again, he smiled apologetically. "I'm sorry. I didn't mean to embarrass you by getting all emotional on our first meeting. It's just that I love her too much to see her suffer. Even the thought overwhelms me…" Siya looked down at her feet, not knowing what to say, as silence descended on them.

Just then, Manoj walked up to them, his drink refreshed. "So, what were we talking about?" he asked Neel.

Neel jumped at the opportunity to change the mood of the conversation. "We were going to talk about the kind of funding you will need to launch your company," he said, smugly.

"Aah. . .that sounds like music to my ears. But, I'm afraid we'll be boring Siya with money talk. Right, Siya?" he asked, politely.

"I agree," Neel said with practiced enthusiasm.

"Don't worry about me. I'll go and catch up with Aisha. Please carry on chatting." *Can a man love a woman so much that he would express it so openly in front of a stranger? I wonder what Samar would do if I went into depression,* she thought as she turned away from them, her eyes searching the living room, resting on Samar.

Aisha wanted to know how Siya's conversation went with Manoj. Siya gave her a low down and informed Aisha that she had to send him a sample write-up. "Did you guys talk numbers?" Aisha also wanted to know.

"Nope, too early for that, I think. However, I did tell him that I'm not interested in selling ad space, Aisha."

"Good. Always better to clarify. Come now, have some of this grilled fish—I had it made keeping your diet in mind."

"Thank you so much, darling!" Siya said, beaming at her.

Later that night, as they were getting ready to crash, Samar said "Great couple. Neel seems like a nice guy with good taste."

"Yeah. I found the décor of the house a bit impersonal but I guess different strokes for different folks. The best thing about him, though, is how much he loves Aisha."

Samar stopped to look at her. "He told you that?" Siya narrated her conversation with Neel and his reaction. "He's a...what do you call them? The SRK type of guys... Metrosexual man!"

"What rubbish! He loves his wife very much and he's not embarrassed to show it. I think that's very cute," said Siya, whacking him playfully with her hairbrush as she continued to comb her hair.

"Siya, normal men don't go around telling their wife's friends how much they love her. There are other ways to express it!"

"Really? Like what?" she asked, turning away from the mirror to face him. Pulling her into his arms, he looked into her eyes and said, "Let me show you."

21

Siya sent a message to Aisha the next morning, thanking her for the lovely evening.

G'morning! We had a really nice evening yesterday. Everything was lovely—your house, the food and wine but most of all, your husband! I'm so happy that you have found such a loving man. Hugs!

She didn't hear back from Aisha all day. *That's ok…it's the weekend, she must be busy; just as I am.*

On Sunday evening, she got a message from Maya: *Hi, Siya! How are you? It seems like ages since I last saw you. Coffee at 11 am on Monday good with you? Maya.*

S: *That would be lovely, Maya! Looking forward. Gloria Jeans okay with you? Siya.*

M: *Sure! See you there. Love. Maya.*

"I'm going to meet Maya for coffee today. Anything you want me to convey to her?" Siya asked Samar as he was having his breakfast the next morning.

"Not really. I'm in touch with Imran. We must call them home some time, Siya. It's been a while…"

"You're right. With all this moving, settling in and dieting, I've stopped thinking of inviting people over."

"I'd warned you earlier. Don't lose focus of other things."

"I know. I have been absorbed with it but that's how I am. I can't do too many things at one time. Anyway, let's not argue first thing in the morning. Now that I know how to manage my diet responsibly, I will ask Maya for a date that suits them both. We'll have them over soon," she said, reaching out to plant a kiss on his cheek. "I'll just change and come with you. Drop me to the gym, please."

"You're going early today?"

"Yeah, I have to meet Maya at eleven, so I need to be back home by ten at least."

As Siya and Samar were waiting for the elevator to arrive, Ira stepped out of her apartment. "Oh, hi guys!" she said, beaming at Samar, as she took in his appearance. "You look dapper in a suit, Samar!" she said, as Samar blushed.

"Thank you! It's just work wear."

"I wouldn't have quit work if I had such handsome men working in my office," she continued, totally impervious to how uncomfortable she was making Siya. As they travelled together in the elevator, Ira made conversation only with Samar about how more players were joining the aviation business, totally ignoring Siya.

When they finally parted ways in the lobby, Siya exhaled. "That woman is too much," she said as soon they'd seated themselves in their car, which was waiting at the porch.

"She was just enquiring about my work, making polite conversation," said Samar, in a small voice.

"Oh yeah? 'I wouldn't have quit if there were handsome men like you in my office' is not polite conversation."

"Don't overreact, Siya! She's just outspoken and bold. Sometimes, I wish you were too," he said, muttering under his breath as he looked away.

Fuming with anger, Siya didn't utter a word as they drove to the gym. When the driver stopped at the gym building, Siya gathered her bag and alighted. Slamming the door shut with a bang, she tried to infuse as much agitation into it as she could. *Idiot. He wants me to be like her. Like her? He will never be able to live with someone like her...she's so full of herself. She won't make any compromises or pander to his needs like I do...it'll probably end in a divorce sooner or later.*

When one is bristling with anger, a gym is the best place to be. It helps you channelise all the negative energy into pushing yourself harder. You find that you can lift extra weights or run that extra kilometre effortlessly. "Ma'am, today you're in very good form! *Kya khaa ke aaye ho*?" asked Ajay with a cheeky smile, as she finished a set of bench presses with thirty kilos of weight on the bar.

Wiping the sweat from her brow, she smiled at him. "*Gussa* (anger). That's what I had before coming here," she said, with a sombre expression.

The smile faded from his face as he looked on. "Aah... then you've come to the right place. Your anger will melt to make you fitter. Do another set of bench press and move fast," he said, thumping her on the back.

Walking back home from the gym, Siya felt exhausted but cleansed of all the anger. *Ajay was right—the gym is the best place to go when you are angry. If I meet Ira more often, I could actually achieve my weight loss goals in half the time!*

She got home and checked her laptop at the dining table as she waited for Vaishali to serve her breakfast. There was a new message.

I understand completely, Siya. I don't want to 'rock the boat' either. I just got so excited seeing a message from you. I've been with the Army since I left college. I've travelled all over the country on my postings. I've lived in Pune, Bhopal, Aurangabad… I'm single but my parents live with me now.

Siya beamed. *He got excited seeing a message from me! And, he's a bachelor…methinks he didn't find anyone better! You should have known, Siddhant Malhotra.*

Tucking into her bowl of oats porridge, Siya re-read the message. She started composing a response as she read along… *Not yet. Let me read this a couple of times before replying. Besides, I don't want him to think I'm too eager or desperate. I have to play it cool.*

With a small smile playing on her lips, Siya finished breakfast and got ready. Dressed in a sleeveless white cotton top and a yellow, fish cut skirt that reached her calves; Siya attracted a few appreciative looks as she alighted from her car fifteen minutes later at Gloria Jeans. It was packed with people even at 11 am. *I didn't know Indians love coffee so much!* "Siya, over here!" she heard a voice calling. She turned around and saw Maya ensconced in a corner booth. Walking towards the table, Siya admired Maya's perfectly blow-dried hair and beautiful features. Maya extricated herself from the booth and came forward to hug her warmly.

"You have lost weight since I last saw you, Siya! You are looking radiant and fit," she said, planting a kiss on her cheek.

"Thank you, Maya. It's so good to know that my effort is visible to everyone else too."

"Well, you're the best judge of your success because you know the *inside story!* How many kilos have you lost?"

"I've lost five so far, another ten to go!"

"Wow! Five kilos is not easy. I'm so proud of you. How's the family been? Supportive? Wait. Before you answer that, let's place our orders," she said, handing Siya a menu to browse.

Siya studied the menu pensively for a while. "I never know what to order in a coffee shop. I don't enjoy coffee and they don't serve a decent cup of tea," she fretted.

"There are some teas here...look, green tea, chamomile, Assam," Maya pointed out.

"I don't like this teabag *wali* chai... Why can't one get a cup of brewed tea at these fancy cafes despite being a tea drinking nation!" she grumbled.

"Oh, I didn't know you are so particular about your tea. I would have invited you home," Maya tried to pacify her.

"Don't worry, I'm just ranting... I've had my stipulated one cup this morning. I'll try something else," she said, trying to sound enthusiastic. "I'll have the sugar-free mixed berry blast! What about you, Maya?"

"Oh, it's a foregone conclusion for me—Americano!"

As soon as the orders were placed, the two women plunged into a discussion about their husbands and kids, workout and food myths and Bombay. Maya was an attentive listener and Siya found herself sharing titbits about her everyday life and feelings without any reserve. "You're so easy to talk to, Maya. I haven't met anyone like you."

"Oh, that's so sweet of you. But, the credit for that goes to Imran. I've learnt so much from watching him deal with people. He's gentle and kind to people when they talk. Of course, that encourages them to talk a lot more than they intend to which is why his sessions always run over the allotted time!"

"Hahaha! You're lucky to have a therapist right at home then!"

"You're so right about that. I can tell him anything at all because I know he won't judge me. When I'm in a dilemma, he helps me to break down my emotions till I arrive at the root. Once I know the cause, I try to resolve it," her eyes had a far-away look as her voice trailed off.

"How lucky that you can tell him anything without any hesitation. I wish I could do the same with mine."

"I'm sure you can! Samar is such a nice guy, Imran is very fond of him. Clear hearted and genuine is how he describes him."

"Imran is absolutely right there but sometimes, Samar can be brutally critical. Like this morning..." and Siya narrated what had transpired between them, thanks to their catty neighbour.

Maya reasoned calmly and sensibly, "Men cannot resist a woman who pays them attention, especially if she isn't his wife. It massages their ego. She sounds harmless to me, Siya. Her bark is probably worse than her bite. You need to find someone who will massage your ego! Tell you things that your husband doesn't. Simple." Siya looked at Maya. She had an impish smile on her face. Maya smiled back. "What? What is it? Tell me?" Maya demanded.

"Nothing," Siya answered, still grinning.

"You can tell me, Siya. I won't tell anyone. God promise, cross my heart," she said, crossing over her heart. Siya laughed. And, it all came tumbling out...the nudge to re-connect from Aisha and the latest email she had received just that morning. "Well, good for you. But, I would suggest that you mention it to Samar oh-so-casually that he doesn't pay much attention to it. And, of course, keep it breezy and light with your ex; you don't want him thinking you are a desperate housewife!"

"Of course, not! Every time I write to him, I read it many times over to ensure it sounds proper. I've only written to him once so far. But, tell me, it's not wrong, is it?"

Maya smiled. "What matters is not what you think or feel now. What's important is what you do with it. Ultimately, your actions will affect you. So, think before you act."

"Don't be so cryptic, Maya! You're sounding like your husband now…," Siya bemoaned.

Maya placed her hand on Siya's in a reassuring gesture and said, "It's not wrong. I know you…you're sensible."

Siya was in better spirits after meeting Maya. Even when she was watching her favourite TV show later, she could not focus and her thoughts kept running amok. *I'm not doing anything wrong. Maya herself said that. It's just an exchange of emails, like the 'pen pals' of yore… Except that you have known him more intimately than pen pals do. Yeah, but I'm not looking for a relationship! I'm a happily married woman… Then, what are you looking for? Haven't you burnt your fingers once? Don't tread into unfamiliar territory, Siya. What will Samar think when he gets to know? But, I'm not going to hide it from him! I will tell him…what? That you are re-establishing contact with your ex? Which man will take it lightly? His question to you will be—why, Siya? Why now? Am I not enough?* The pinging of her cell phone broke into her reverie. It was a message from Aisha. She put the TV on mute as she read it.

Hi! I'm sorry I didn't respond to your SMS earlier. I'm glad you guys enjoyed yourselves; it was lovely meeting Samar too.

Siya re-read the message, in a daze. She was trying to escape the thoughts that ricocheted in her mind so she could make sense of Aisha's message. She typed out her answer...

Next time around, let's meet at our place!

And then she remembered Neel's revelation about Aisha's depression. *Should I ask her about it? I don't think so... wait for her to tell you herself. If she believes you need to know and she's comfortable enough disclosing it.*

She remembered that she also had to invite Maya and Imran for dinner. She messaged her asking for a date.

Maya replied almost immediately acknowledging the message and confirming that she would get back with a suitable date.

Siya smiled to herself and then went back to agonising if she should reply to Siddhant's message or wait a while. Since she wasn't able to make up her mind, she re-read his message instead!

22

Having waited a full six hours, Siya was eager to send off her reply to Siddhant. *I should refrain from making any references to his single status.*

Your life seems so exciting—just what the doctor ordered! You've travelled and lived in so many different places. The only cities I have known are Delhi and Mumbai! So, what do you do in the Army every day? What's an average day in a soldier's life like? Do share.

Siya sat back and read her message, doubly checking if it was safe to send. Just then Samar called. Recalling their argument that morning, she answered in a tone devoid of affection or warmth. "Hey, what are you doing?" he asked, in a cheerful tone.

"Writing to an old boyfriend," she said, with glee.

"Really? Which one? You had so many…" his voice trailed off.

"The only one who mattered…," she said, in a small voice.

"What was his name? Siddhartha? Siddhant?" he probed.

"Siddhant," she said.

"I hope he's doing well," said Samar, after a pause.

"Yes, he is. He's in the Army, you know…"

"Aah, that's good. Ok, listen I called to tell you that I've spoken with Imran. They are free for dinner next weekend. Would you like to invite anyone else? I'll leave it to you to plan the rest of the details. See you later. Bye," he hung up abruptly.

Siya was nonplussed. *That was easy… Did it irk him? Did he even believe me? Or, did he think I was deliberately vexing him? He didn't seem keen to talk about it. Maybe, he was in the middle of something and had just called to convey the message about dinner…anyway, I've told him oh-so-casually now. Thank God I got that out of the way.*

At dinner that evening, Siya was very quiet. Samar noticed that she was not paying attention. "Are you still mad about what I said to you this morning?" he asked.

Siya was confused. *He thinks I'm still mad at him and here I am, thinking he is distant because of…* "Well, it was uncalled for. I didn't like being compared."

"I know, I realise that wasn't fair. But, why are you so insecure around her? Why do you just clam shut?" This triggered an immediate response and the air around the table got pensive as Samar and Siya argued.

23

Siya started working on her first piece for Manoj at *Powai Info*. Since he hadn't given her a specific topic to write on but nudged her towards the subject of 'children', she spent some time mulling over it.

One afternoon, as she sat browsing the TV while waiting for the kids to come home, she stopped at a channel where a group of overly made up children were competing in a singing competition. She was aghast. *Oh my God, this little girl is only seven years old! Look at her makeup and outfit. Judging by her mannerisms and demeanour, she could pass off as an adult! And, that boy—only ten years old but what a melodious voice! Wait a minute, shouldn't he be in school right now? I wonder if he's doing this of his own volition or being forced to. His parents seem like lower middle class…who knows. But, that girl comes from a reasonably well-off family. I wonder what her reasons are for missing school. Don't these kids want to watch cartoons or play with their friends in their free time? Which kid would give that up for this? Sigh…*

She immediately got up to do some research. Siya was astounded to see how children were everywhere on Indian television—from family soaps to music and dance extravaganzas. Most of the kids were from five to fifteen years old. *What does a child even know at five? Isn't this a form of abuse? At fifteen, a child may know but can still be coerced into doing things. Or, could they? I should talk to some of the school mums who have teenage kids. They could tell me. What else can I do?*

Siya was excited at the prospect of writing a story on something she had idly wondered about at times. She decided to speak to Imran and get his view on the subject as well.

She had finally figured what her sample-write up was to be on.

Having spent two days researching the topic had left Siya feeling low and helpless. *I wish I could drive some sense into these people. The damage they are doing to their kids is irreversible.* She decided to message Aisha and speak to her.

Siya: *Hi! Are you free to meet up some time? I really need a pick me up.*

Aisha: *I'm sorry I can't. Have hurt my back badly. It's really painful. Need to rest up.*

S: *Oh, that's awful! How did that happen?*

A: *Don't ask…it was an accident.*

S: *Can I do anything to help? Please tell me.*

A: *Thank you, sweety. I've seen the doctor and am on painkillers. Will message you when I'm feeling better.*

S: *Sure. Take care and I hope you feel better real soon.*

Siya opened the document on her laptop and started working on it.

You have one new message from Siddhant Shankar—flashed on the top of her laptop screen.

Siya smiled. *Now, here's someone I can talk to about my current mood.* She quickly scanned the write up for any grammatical mistakes, re-read the beginning and end and emailed it. She couldn't wait to log in and read his message. *Wonder if it's a long one. Siya, stop behaving like a teenager!* Siya smiled as the message opened up…it was reasonably long!

Well, my life is not as exciting as it sounds. We don't walk around toting guns in a Rambo-like fashion! An average day for me starts at 5 am with a jog or run followed by administrative work in the office during the day. The evenings generally find me playing a sport with my buddies till it's time to hit the bar! Drinking leads to eating and that's when the sun sets for me generally. Nothing to envy there, eh? What about you? What do you do all day long? How do you spend your time? Tell me what you like to do.

Siya smiled again. He wanted to know what she liked to do and how she spent her time. It had been so long since she had thought about those things herself.

It does sound kind of rough—your everyday life. But, I could do with a couple of days like that every now and then. My life here is so full of activity that sometimes, the hours seem less. Between running home and taking care of my husband and kids, I have to also make time for my workout (be it yoga or weights or cardio) and some amount of socialising. I have recently started writing. In fact, I've just spent the last couple of days researching on how children are exploited by media and television. It has affected me deeply. I cannot comprehend why parents would do it to their own innocent kids. We have our whole life to be adults but once your childhood years pass by, you can never be a child again. It's gone forever.

Oh gosh, I've been ranting! Hope you don't mind that. It's just that these thoughts have been weighing on my mind so I couldn't help myself.

More later. Bye!

She pressed Send and immediately regretted sending such a long rant, that too about children. He was a single man and had no kids.

Siya received a call from Manoj that evening; she wasn't sure what to expect when she saw his name flash on the screen. "Siya, I loved your piece!"

"Really?"

"Yes! It's just the kind of topic we need to get the community involved. It will lead to a lot of discussion and debate. I'm looking forward to the traffic my website will receive!"

"Wow! I'm getting excited just listening to your enthusiasm. I'm so glad you like it... I wasn't sure if you'd empathise, considering you're single now," Siya blurted out.

"I'm divorced, Siya, but I do have a son so technically, I'm still a parent."

Oh no, how can you say that, Siya? You and your big mouth... "I'm so sorry I didn't mean it that way. I didn't know..."

"No offence taken, Siya! I like that you speak your mind, even if inadvertently. Makes it easy to work with people who say what's on their mind—clears the air."

"I didn't mean to make it awkward for you. I tend to put my foot in my mouth sometimes but it's without malice."

Manoj mentioned he would post the article the next day and asked her for an author introduction. She was zapped. *Author?* She asked Manoj what she should put in her introduction—she was a stay-at-home mom. Manoj asked her to put that and list some of her interests and asked her to send it to him by evening.

Siya ended the call, savouring the feeling. *I'm an author now! Gosh, I can't wait to tell Samar! I'll ask him what to write for the author introduction; he'll know exactly what I should put.* She picked up her phone again, beaming at the screen, as she typed a message to Samar.

When are you coming home? Have something to share.

She had just sent the message when her phone rang. It was Samar! *I knew it. He just can't wait; he has to know now.* "What's up, Siya? All ok?" he asked as soon as she answered.

"Yes! Don't worry, I'm not pregnant. All is well, Samar," and then she narrated her conversation with Manoj. Samar assured her that she was capable of writing an author introduction which he would read when he got home.

The next day at noon, Siya received a message from Manoj that the article had been posted. Siya immediately logged into *Powai Info*—there it was.

Let's Save Our Children's Childhood

By Siya Rai Chowdhary

Siya couldn't believe it. *Seeing one's name in print is such a heady feeling!* She decided to visit Aisha and thank her in person, after all she was the one who had given her the idea and introduced her to Manoj.

24

Siya teamed a pair of white denim capris with a navy blue and white striped, fitted top as she got ready to visit Aisha. Looking at her reflection in the mirror, she thought, *Wow! You have lost weight! You're looking really slim! Thank you, dear God.*

Stopping at a florist on the way, she picked up a bunch of pink and white carnations. As she stepped out of her car in the lobby of Octavius, Siya was struck by how new and white it was. When the guard enquired after her name, she gave it and said in the same breath, "Please don't tell ma'am I'm here. It's a surprise," pointing to the flowers in her hand. He smiled as he picked up the intercom and pointed her towards the lifts.

The door was opened by a young Maharashtrian girl, dressed fashionably in jeans. The girl ushered her into Aisha's bedroom where she lay on her bed with her eyes closed. Just like the living and dining room, her bedroom was contemporary in décor but minimalist in design.

Aisha looked up at the sound of voices and smiled at Siya. She was happy to see the pretty flowers and asked Siya to sit in a chair next to the bed. Siya asked her how she had hurt her back. "Did it happen in the gym?" Aisha nodded sheepishly. She was amused by Siya's questions and concern but assured her that her back would heal soon.

"I'm going to undergo a course of ayurvedic treatment as a follow up thereafter. It was not the trainer's fault; I was pushing myself, testing my strength. He wasn't even around, Siya."

"You stupid girl! Who were you trying to impress? I'm sure there must have been some hunk around!" Siya claimed as she playfully whacked at her hand.

"How did you know?" Aisha kidded. "Sometimes, you have to stretch your limits to attract certain people," Aisha continued, sombrely.

"You are a mother of two. I think you have stretched yourself enough. You don't need to impress anyone that badly," Siya said, placing her hand on Aisha's cheek. A tear ran down the length of Aisha's face. Her eyes glistened.

"What's the matter, darling? Why are you crying?" Siya was taken aback.

"I'm not used to people sympathising with me," she answered, in a small voice.

"Story of our lives, isn't it? Nobody sees how much it takes to keep things together. It's our fault actually, we make it look like a cakewalk!" Siya answered, trying to inject a happy tone in her voice.

"*You* make it look like a cakewalk while I struggle with it," Aisha answered in protest.

"Oh, what nonsense. You have a husband who loves you so much. I'm sure that is because of who you are and what you do," Siya argues.

Aisha smiled feebly and brushed away her tears. She then called her help on her iPhone and asked her to make some green tea for both of them. As soon as she had finished giving instructions and hung up, Siya told her about her article in *Powai Info*. Aisha was immediately interested and wanted to see the piece. Siya helped her to sit up in bed as she arranged four pillows to support her back. Even though Aisha was in pain, she wanted to read the piece.

As she pored over the write up with concentration, Siya caught the changing expressions on Aisha's face. Consternation, sadness, anger…ending with a small smile, directed at Siya. "Well written, Siya! You've put your points across with great conviction. It's obviously something you feel strongly about."

Siya smiled. "How well you know me."

Over cups of green tea, they spent the morning talking more about the write up, among other things. "Aisha, I took your advice and re-connected with an ex college mate," Siya said, after a while.

Aisha looked up at her. "And?"

"And, we've been writing to each other on and off, about everyday stuff; taking care to stay away from personal things. It makes me nervous sometimes… I'm afraid I'll say something innocuous that may be misconstrued. I have to be careful with my words."

"That seems stressful—having to think before you say, I mean write."

"It is, at times. On the other hand, I'm enjoying the whole process of writing, sending it off and waiting for a reply. It makes me feel like a teenager in love!" Siya sighed.

"Well, are you?"

"Am I what?"

"In love with him?"

"Aisha! No, I'm not…how can you even think that? In fact, I'm not sure I ever was. I think the notion of having a lover is more enchanting than actually loving someone, especially when you are young. Love requires a lot of work, it doesn't strike like lightning as we've been made to believe. Physical attraction is what draws you to a person. Love grows with time."

"Then, why did you reach out to him?" Aisha challenged Siya.

"Let's just say I needed an ego booster. Husbands don't always say the things we want to hear, do they?"

"Do you love your husband?" Aisha asked.

"Of course, I love Samar!"

"Were you attracted to him from the beginning?" she persevered.

"Yes, I was! That's a silly question, Aisha," said Siya, trying not to be upset with her friend. "What's the matter, Aisha?" she asked gently, placing a hand on hers.

"Nothing," said Aisha, in an exasperated tone. "I just have so much time on my hands, now that I am immobile, that my mind wanders... I'm sorry, I didn't mean to be nosy," she implored, taking her palm in her hands.

"Don't be stupid. That's not what I meant. Why don't you read some good books? Or, watch some funny movies? Let me know if you want me to bring some over. We could watch it together," Siya said, trying to make peace.

Aisha looked at her in silence, as if weighing her thoughts. "What is it, Aisha? Is something bothering you?" she asked.

Aisha sighed. "Siya, I reconnected with my ex too; a couple of years ago, actually."

"Oh...and?" she asked.

"I'm still in love with him," she said, simply.

"But, Aisha..."

"I know what you are going to say. I have a husband and kids. I should not think of other men. But, I don't love Neel, Siya," and she burst into tears. Siya was stunned. She sat next to Aisha on the bed, hugging her tentatively so as to not hurt her back. Tears racked Aisha's body gently. Siya uttered words of comfort while patting her head with one hand.

After a few minutes, Aisha's body stilled and she pulled away from Siya. "I'm sure you have a lot to do while the kids are in school" she remarked, sniffing as she wiped away her tears.

"Aisha, I don't have to do anything else. Do you want to talk?" she asked.

"No. I'm tired actually. I want to rest a bit now, if you don't mind," she said, dismissing Siya gently. Siya felt hurt at being cut off like that. She tried to reassure Aisha, "Please let me know if you need anything. I'm always here for you." Aisha smiled back at her as she nodded and left the apartment.

Siya felt sorry for Aisha and the turmoil she was in. She hoped that this was a passing phase and worried how Aisha coped with all the emotions raging within. *Guilt itself can kill you,* she thought. She so wanted to reach out and help her.

That evening, when Samar walked in, Siya was sitting in her room on the lazy chair, with her gaze fixed at some point on the wall in front. She had not been able to stop thinking about what Aisha had said. *Neel loves her so much...why does she not love him equally? Why has she been living with him all these years? Does Neel know she loves someone else? Is it possible to live with one person while loving another? Or, is it just mid-life crisis? Would some sort of counselling help her?*

"Where is my favourite writer?" the sound of Samar's booming voice, broke into her reverie. She stood up at the sound of his voice.

"Wow!" she exclaimed as he walked in, holding out a bunch of red roses for her. "These are beautiful, Samar! And, they smell perfect" she said, inhaling their sweet smell with satisfaction. "What's the occasion?" she asked, opening the card that was attached. 'For my writer wife'—it said. Siya couldn't stop grinning from ear to ear! "But, you haven't even read the write up yet! Come, let me show you," she said, opening up the laptop and turning the face of the screen towards him.

Siya sat on the bed and watched him read it. His face was impassive; not expressive like Aisha's. "Nicely done, Siya! This is good stuff" he said, after five long minutes.

"Really? You're not saying that just because you are married to this writer?"

"Well, I wouldn't have read it otherwise! You know how much I read...," he said, hugging her as his lips found hers. "Why don't we celebrate?" he asked, pulling away from her.

"I thought that's what we were doing!" Siya said, a twinkle in her eyes.

"Oh, this is not even the tip of the iceberg, madam. We shall do much more than this!" Siya beamed at him. "Let's go away for a weekend. Just relax and unwind."

Oh...I hope I can access Facebook! Wait a minute, where did that come from? "Which place do you have in mind?" she asked.

"Let's go to the new hotel in Aamby Valley, ahead of Lonavala. I hear it's beautifully done."

Hmmm...then it should have internet. Siya, really? "Ok! Let's!" she said, enthusiastically.

Later that night, Samar shared that he had asked Imran and Maya to join them in their getaway. "It'll be good to have company. Besides, our boys will have fun with their kids—they are so well-mannered and sweet"

"Oh, I enjoy Maya's company. It'll be nice to spend more time with Imran too. He is so handsome," Siya said, with an exaggerated sigh.

"That he is. I agree," said Samar, giving her a thumbs up.

"You're not jealous?" Siya asked, incredulously.

"Of my friend, Imran? No way. I don't grudge him for what he has, from nature or otherwise."

"What if I have a crush on him?"

"You would be abnormal if you didn't, Siya. It's natural. He's a very good-looking man."

Siya looked at him, wide eyed. *This is my husband?* "What if I have a crush on someone else?" she asked, challenging him.

"Siya, you are not only my wife but also a human being. I cannot chain your thoughts or feelings...you are free to fantasise about whoever you want; as long as I'm the recipient of your passion."

Now would be a good time to tell him, Siya. "So, what if I told you that I have been in touch with my ex from college?" she asked.

"In person?" he asked.

"No, through Facebook."

"That's what Facebook is for. To connect with people," he stated, matter-of-factly.

"You don't mind that I'm in touch with him?"

"That depends on why you needed to connect," he answered. Siya toyed with the thought of confessing; but before she could say anything he asked, "Is he in a position to help you professionally?" For a minute, Siya wondered what he was talking about. Her confusion was evident on her face. "I mean with your articles and writing stuff," he elaborated.

"Oh! Yes, he has been very helpful actually. He read my article and gave me feedback on how to improve it. I've been in touch with him for that only. We used to be on the college editorial board together!"

"That's perfectly legit then," he stated, calmly. Smiling meekly in acknowledgement, Siya turned around to pick up her book from the bedside table. As her gaze fell on the laptop lying there, she made a mental note to put it away in her cupboard just in case...

Delhi, July 1994

Because I love you—Shakin Stevens

"Meet me at the Mehra Family Clinic in Punjabi Bagh tomorrow morning at nine." Didi said as she explained the directions to me. I heaved a sigh of relief and burst into tears as I clutched the receiver to my ears. I didn't realise how tense I had been. I would have an adult with me in case... better not think about that now.

The next morning, I got ready to go to work as usual. I wondered if anyone sensed anything...nothing was said so I assumed they didn't. I left home at eight o'clock, factoring in travel time plus time to locate the nursing home as I had never been there. I wanted to get it over and done with, as soon as possible.

Didi was waiting at the reception, looking anxious. I managed to keep my emotions in check as she hugged me. Thank God she didn't talk about the problem at hand. I needed someone to hold my hand then, not to reprimand me. I had to be brave, for me.

The doctor was a kind little woman...petite with a crop of silver-grey hair. Delicate, gold-rimmed spectacles adorned her wizened face as she smiled at me, sympathetically. To my utter relief, she didn't ask me any questions. Didi had obviously briefed her. "I wish youngsters would use contraception," she tut-tutted as she signalled for me to lie down for a physical exam.

"You're in good hands, it'll be over soon," said my sister, hugging me before leaving the room.

The doctor poked and probed my vagina to be doubly sure that a procedure was required. "I will send the nurse in to prep you for the procedure," she said, after the physical exam.

A uniformed nurse, dark-complexioned with curly black hair, entered the room soon after. She informed me that once I was undressed, she would shave off my pubic hair. I nodded mutely as the incongruity of the situation struck me. I, who had never had my bikini line waxed because I felt shy and awkward, was in no position to protest! After finishing her task, the nurse informed me that the doctor would be with me soon. As the minutes ticked, I wondered: Will I live through this?

Just then, the doctor entered the room and gently explained the procedure to be followed. I would be given anaesthesia so I could sleep through it. "What if I don't wake up, doctor?" I asked, trembling at the thought. She smiled reassuringly and rubbished my fears. I smiled timidly, grateful for her presence. As I got ready for the procedure, awkward, exposed and vulnerable, she took my hand and squeezed it softly.

"Your sister wanted me to tell you that she is waiting outside for you. Don't worry, it will be all right. Just relax." That was the last instruction I heard before going into a deep sleep.

I woke up in a dark, cool room. Didi was sitting by my bedside. As I tried to sit up, she came forward to help me. "It's done now. But, you have to promise me that you are never going to see that boy again..."

"But, Didi..."

"No buts. This is the only thing that boys want. Don't you get it? They are all the same, however decent they may look and whatever families they come from," she added, emphatically.

"He's not like that. He never forced me...we were in it together."

"Nonsense. What together? His life hasn't been affected at all. Where is he now, when you are in the trouble that he has put you in? Give up on these stupid romantic ideas. Thank God you told me before anybody else. Anything could have gone wrong. What if, what if...just don't meet him anymore. Promise me, please," Didi said as she hugged me and tears streamed down my face.

25

Driving down the Mumbai-Pune Expressway just as the monsoon hits is so exhilarating! The Western Ghats are verdant green and everything looks like it's being given a makeover! The breeze is cool and crisp, the birds chirpy and delighted.

As more clouds gathered around, their cars started climbing upwards from Lonavala. Although mist and fog made visibility poor, the two cars steadily drove on humming along to the music of RD and lyrics of Gulzar on the radio. When they reached the top, also known as Tiger's Point, they decided to take a small break, stretch their legs and take photos of the breath-taking views all around. There's nothing more uplifting than the rains!

They arrived at Aamby Valley by noon, after negotiating a couple of hairpin bends. The towering gates of the hotel were opened by smartly uniformed men. After a thorough security check of their cars and bags, they were allowed to drive to the reception which was housed in a wooden chalet, built out of logs. Samar let out a low whistle as he drove into the porch. "Wow! This is more than what I expected," he announced.

"It is so posh and charming, at the same time," Siya remarked. Disembarking from their cars, the boys were excited at having arrived at their destination finally! As Maya gave instructions to the staff on handling the baggage, the menfolk dealt with the formalities of check in at the reception.

"Our rooms have been allotted, folks. Let's freshen up and get together for lunch." Samar stated, pulling Arjun into his arms to cuddle. "You'll feel okay soon, baby. The fresh air will do you good." Arjun's eyes lit up when he saw the golf carts that would take them to their rooms! He scrambled out of Samar's arms and joined the older kids, their excitement getting to him eventually. As they were driven to their rooms, they gasped in unison at the winding pathways lined with trees, thick with foliage. There were wooden chalets everywhere.

"Papa, are these our rooms?" Aryan asked.

"Yes, young man. Your rooms are inside these chalets," their driver answered.

"Yes!" Aryan exclaimed, pumping his fist in the air, with a broad grin on his face. Arjun looked at him and smiled excitedly. In the distance, they could see a huge lake along the path they were travelling.

"What lake is that?" Samar asked their driver.

"That's an artificial lake, sir," he replied.

"Wow! Really? That's marvellous," he exclaimed.

The golf cart stopped at a set of twin chalets. The adults laughed as all four boys jumped out and ran to explore the inside of the chalets. "Papa, this is like the Bears' home in Goldilocks!" shrieked Arjun from inside.

Imran patted Samar on his back. "Good choice, *dost*," he said.

"I know. I'm pleasantly surprised myself. I haven't seen accommodation of this standard in these parts before," Samar answered.

The chalet was split into two levels. The ground floor had one master bed alongside a small lounge area. An open kitchenette with a high breakfast table, akin to a bar, separated the lounge from the bed. It was completely made up of wooden logs. "My God, this is so beautiful! Thank you so much, Samar. This is perfect," said Siya, giving him a peck on his cheek. As she drew the curtain aside to check out the view, the boys ran into the bathroom to explore.

"Wow! A Jacuzzi, Papa! Come here and see," Aryan called out. Siya smiled at him as he walked towards the bathroom. The balcony was like a deck—all wooden planks. A wrought iron round table with four chairs was placed in the centre. Pulling a chair out to sit, Siya looked outwards—she could only see green lawns and blue skies. The occasional gardener loitered around, watering the flower bushes and birds twittered in the trees.

Everything else was quiet. Siya was tuning her ears to the sounds of silence. *It feels so good to be away from the noise and clamour of the city. So clean and green. I could stay here, forever.* Siya breathed in the smell of rain and freshly cut grass. *Will you be able to access Facebook, Siya?* Her brows furrowed as her senses were distracted. Siya got up abruptly to go in. She retrieved her phone from her handbag and looked at the screen. *No signal, no internet.* She humphed.

"What's the matter?" Samar asked, walking out of the bathroom.

"No signal on my phone," said Siya, holding her phone out for him to see.

Samar looked at the screen and then took out his phone from his pocket. "No signal on mine either. Just switch it off and on, it should work," he said, handing her phone back to her. "By the way, the kids are having a bubble bath. They got so excited with the huge tub that they couldn't resist it," he smiled at her.

The rest of the day passed pleasantly for both the families. As the children explored various activities that the hotel offered, the adults accompanied them, marvelling at the state-of-the-art recreation facilities.

After lunch, they decided to play a round of golf at the driving range as the sky was overcast and a gentle breeze was blowing. While the kids decided to stay indoors and watch TV, the adults set off in a golf cart. As the cart arrived at the PGA 18-hole golf course, Imran let out a whistle. "Boy, this man has style! What a treat this is!" As Samar, Maya and Imran went about procuring their golf kits (Siya didn't play golf), Siya admired the limitless expanse of green. *If the skies turn grey anymore then it could rain. What fun it would be to walk in the rain!*

As the others teed off, Siya wandered into the adjoining lounge cum bar. It was built like a man's den. It had the signature logwood interior but was furnished with leather sofas and couches. The walls were lined with framed photos of landmark golf tournaments and memorabilia. Siya walked around for a bit but soon got tired with all the golf trivia. Taking a seat on one of the wingback leather chairs, she fished out her phone from her handbag. She'd managed to get a signal and also find out the login for the hotel wi-fi. *Thank God…it would have been difficult to live in suspense for the entire weekend.* After checking on her email (nothing consequential there), she logged into Facebook to see what her community of virtual friends were up to.

As soon as she logged in, she saw the red blob on top of the Messages icon. She had one message. *But, I only wrote to him two days ago. Has he already replied?* Clicking on the icon, she opened her message box and there it was—a reply from him! Looking around to make sure Samar wasn't watching, she clicked on the message to read it. Suddenly, the application closed on her phone, leaving her confused. *Huh, what happened?* She opened the app again and clicked on her message box. The screen went black and the home screen showed up. Siya looked around to see if there was anyone who could help. *Just when I have a message to read, the damn phone doesn't work.* She checked the wi-fi settings on her phone—not connected. No 3G either. *I should get to a wi-fi zone somehow. Let me ask at the reception.* Exiting the lounge, she approached the gentleman behind the reception of the golf club. "Excuse me, do you have a wi-fi connection here?" she asked.

"Sorry, ma'am; wi-fi connection is very weak here," he said.

"Oh...where can I get a good connection?" she persisted.

"You will have to go to the main reception, ma'am."

"Ok. Can you call for a golf cart to take me there now?" she asked.

"I'm sorry, ma'am, the golf carts are busy with a group check in at the reception right now."

"Oh no. So, when can it come here?" she asked, her irritation reflecting in her tone.

"In thirty or forty minutes, ma'am."

"Ridiculous! You expect me to wait till then?" she asked thunderously, making the man at the reception cower.

Just then, Imran walked in. "Hey, what's the matter, Siya? All okay?" Siya looked behind him, expecting Samar to follow. "They're going to take some more time," he answered, pre-empting her question. His questioning gaze prompted her to say, "There are no golf carts available to take me to the main reception. It'll take at least thirty minutes."

"Have you left something in the room? All okay with the kids?" he asked in a concerned tone.

"Yeah, the kids are okay. It's just that I need wi-fi and their connection is no good here," she replied in a small voice.

"We should be done in half an hour, if it can wait. Do you need to check something urgently?"

"No, it's not urgent... I can wait," Siya answered, feeling chastised. *He is a psychologist. Could he have guessed why I'm so antsy?*

"Great! We can all go together then. Why don't you pick up a book to read or have a drink in the meanwhile?" he suggested, as if talking to a child. Siya smiled, half-heartedly, trying to mask her disappointment at not getting what she really wanted.

Sure enough, the golfing trio were back in thirty minutes. "Hey, Siya, hope you didn't get bored here," asked Maya the moment she saw her.

"Not at all. I picked up a book from their lounge and your husband kindly ordered a drink for me," said Siya, smiling at them.

"Aah...the psychologist thinks a drink is the cure for boredom!" she remarked, giving Imran a tight hug.

"Not at all. It's a great accompaniment to a good book!" he answered, mischievously.

"Let's head back to our rooms now," said Samar to the golf cart driver the moment they were seated in it.

"No. Let's go to the reception first," Imran interjected.

"Reception? But why?" he asked.

"Siya wanted to..."

"No, it's okay. Let's just go back to our rooms," said Siya, interrupting Imran. He gave her a quizzical look.

"The kids have been alone for a while," Siya added, hoping that would explain it.

"Okay," said Imran, falling in line, albeit slightly confused.

Alighting at their chalets ten minutes later, they decided to meet for drinks before heading to the laser show. The kids were sprawled out on the bed, watching TV with a glazed look in their eyes as Samar and Siya walked in. Arjun got up and ran to hug Siya while Samar snuggled in bed, next to Aryan. Although her mind was buzzing with thoughts, Siya lay down on the bed with the kids. The gin and tonic had made her languorous and soon, she was swept away into dreamland.

26

They met for drinks later that evening; where Siya stuck to vodka, continuing steadfastly with her diet. She had managed to lose ten kilos in twelve weeks but now it was becoming tedious!

After one round of drinks, they headed to the lakefront to watch the laser show. The children had hopped into a buggy by themselves, excited to beat them to the location!

People were milling at the steps leading down to the lakefront. Everybody had taken a seat on the steps in an amphitheatre style. It was like a picnic minus the food. There were families with kids and grandparents. Some couples walked around hand in hand, looking for a romantic nook where they could enjoy the show, away from prying eyes! A man's voice boomed over a sound system, making the crowd go silent. The next thirty minutes passed in pin-drop silence as everybody drank in the spectacular sights and sounds of the laser show, occasionally gasping at the wondrous images. Figures that were the size of mountains were projected in the air above the water's surface. Dragons spewing fire, dancers bedecked in fine costumes, life-like birds and flowers, heritage monuments with a three-dimensional view—a tapestry of rich images enthralled the audience against the ink black night sky. The accompanying soundtrack narrated the story of India's birth leading up to the birth of the company that was responsible for the construction of that mini city where the hotel was located, extolling their visionary CEO. As the show concluded, the chatter commenced. Excited voices were heard recounting some of the visual images, hoping to lock them away in their memories forever.

They decided to watch the next show at 10 pm and agreed to have dinner first. The kids complied as all of them headed to The Woodpecker, a twenty-four-hour restaurant. The restaurant too was constructed entirely with wood. It was large and airy with an open deck overlooking the lake. A gentle breeze blew, as if tugging at them to come have a seat. Seating themselves at a table on the deck, the two families enjoyed a leisurely dinner, amidst chatter and laughter.

An hour later, as everyone headed towards the laser show in the buggy, Siya requested the driver to drop her at the reception. Imran also decided to get off at the reception to check his email. As they waited in the lounge for the sites to load, they resumed an earlier conversation about her diet.

"So Siya, we were talking about you not being able to lose the last couple of kilos despite following your diet plan strictly," he asked, picking up from where they had left.

"Yes," she answered distractedly, eyes glued to the phone screen.

"You know, there are some studies that have put forth the idea of a connection between body fat and our emotional/mental well-being," he declared.

"Really?" Siya asked, looking up from the phone, her interest piqued. "What's the connection?"

"Well, it seems that emotions like low confidence, low self-esteem, loneliness, fear of rejection, fear of criticism, fear of others finding out secrets we bottle up for years can affect weight loss. In most cases, these emotions are not expressed or dealt with in time so they become like undigested food which just sits on our stomach or limbs and refuses to move despite rigorous exercise and the right food." He paused, waiting for her to absorb it.

Realising that he had her full attention, he continued, "Unresolved issues and grudges we harbour with people—could be our family or friends—plague us till they become detrimental to our well-being. It also works against us, jeopardising our best efforts, when we try to achieve our goals."

Siya was captivated by his words. She wondered if she had unresolved issues and whether he thought she had secrets to hide. "So, how does one lose this fat?" she asked, not referring to it as an 'issue'.

"Well, for starters, one needs to obviously work on expressing. Shaking things up a bit helps. Stepping out of your comfort zone to assert oneself in a situation helps, as does refusing to say or do something that you don't agree with. It brings a sense of peace—knowing that I did what I felt or thought was right without caving in to pressure to conform," Imran advised. Siya listened keenly.

"Unresolved issues require some sort of closure in order for us to live without anxiety. We need to internalise...and figure out what will bring us peace and close the issue so we can move on." He paused.

Siya was nonplussed. She had never dwelt on such feelings or thoughts. *Where was the time?* "So, Imran, how will I know which issue needs to be tackled for me to move on and achieve my goals? I mean, as human beings, we have so many relationships—some are natural while others are forged. There's no perfect relationship. We may have differences of opinion or ideology or behaviour which lead to some negative thoughts every now and then. How will I know which one to resolve and overcome?" Siya passionately enquired.

Imran smiled. "It's not any one issue that will suddenly light up the path ahead for you. It has to be a series of actions. Every action will lead to a reaction which will help you bring forth the strength within. Try it. Start with small things. It'll give you the confidence to tackle the big ones," he advised, smiling at her affectionately.

27

The conversation with Imran had kept her awake through the night. Even the next morning, stray thoughts were darting across her mind. Samar lay sprawled across the king-sized bed, snoring gently. Everyone had gone to sleep only by midnight. The kids had been super charged after seeing the laser show the second time around. Samar, Maya, Imran, and Siya had to calm them down so they would sleep. The adults were tired and ready to knock off but the kids were fighting their sleep, tooth and nail. Eventually, all had fallen in.

Siya pondered at length over what Imran had said. The issues she needed to resolve...hmmm, that reminded her of Aisha. *Aisha—I haven't thought about her all weekend until now. I wonder how she will resolve her issues? I wish I could help her. But, relationships aren't so simple to solve. Hurt, anger, love, respect, jealousy, possessiveness, loyalty—are all involved.* She decided to message Aisha and let her know that she was there for her unconditionally. She reached out for her phone on the bedside table. Disconnecting the charging wire, she opened her message folder and typed it out.

She got a reply almost instantly: *Thanks.*

Siya didn't know what to make of the reply. She thought about what it could have meant and whether it was sarcastic. Aisha had probably expected Siya to be more enthusiastic about her disclosure. Siya had been anything but. She had to make her see sense. *How can I agree with her decision to leave her husband and kids because she believes she has reunited with the love of her life? That won't be fair to them. But, what if this is truly right for her? What if this is finally her chance at happiness? If she has to give up everything else for this then how is it wrong? Uff, it's not that simple.* As always, Siya was overthinking—about things not related to her issues, her insecurities.

When they were at the riding stables later that morning, Manoj called. He asked her if she had checked the comments her write-up had received. When she replied in the negative, he informed her that the issue she raised was being discussed in earnest. He applauded her effort, making her feel delighted with herself. Manoj also asked her to start thinking of her next write-up to build on the momentum the first one had generated. Samar had been looking at her. She excitedly conveyed to him the gist of their conversation which naturally made him happy too.

As they drove back home later that day, Siya's mind was buzzing with ideas for her next write up. She didn't want to write anything serious lest it take away attention from the current issue that was being hotly discussed.

One hundred and fifty-seven comments in two days! Siya was overwhelmed when she logged in on her laptop later that night. People were up in arms at the treatment being meted out to some of the kids who acted on television. Poor working conditions, pushy parents, inadequate sleep, compromised schooling, zero play time, ill effects of being under bright lights with makeup caked on their faces—all for a paltry sum. Since Mumbai was home to the film and television industry, some people talked about taking it up with production houses and introducing legislations to protect the interests of these children.

Siya showed the comments to Samar and they discussed some of them at great length.

Later on, she logged into Facebook from the easy chair, keeping an eye on Samar who lay on the bed and excitedly opened Siddhant's message.

I'm so glad you feel comfortable enough to share the thoughts that move you deeply, with me. I feel the same with you. The years have obviously not affected our ease with each other. I have been battling with circumstances too. My parents have been living with me and their health is gradually failing…it is heart wrenching to see them suffer every day. My visions of serving my country heroically have remained just that—dreams. I'm so glad for your friendship, it brings me peace.

On one hand, Siya felt sorry for him but at the same time, she felt avenged. This was poetic justice after all. She had a perfect life in an imperfect world.

28

The next morning, as Siya walked to the gym, she thought of Aisha again and wondered whether to message her or not.

As she walked up to her trainer to begin her workout, she remembered how Aisha had hurt herself in the gym and spoke to him about that. Ajay looked foxed and replied that no one had hurt themselves in this gym. Siya recounted what Aisha had told her, almost accusingly. Out of concern, Ajay spoke to the manager, who had no clue about this incident and asked for details. Siya provided what she knew and passed on Aisha's number. The nervous manager was worried about the negative publicity the gym would receive and hence called Aisha right away.

An hour later, as she walked out of the changing room with her gym bag; the manager approached her and told her that he had spoken to Aisha who told him that her injury was her business and no one else needed to know. When the manager had told Aisha that it was Siya who had given them her number as they wanted to verify facts, Aisha had responded by saying that Siya should mind her own business. Siya was speechless. Tears stung her eyes as she tried to find her voice. She apologised and walked away. As she got into the elevator, her head was buzzing. *Why is Aisha being so catty? Is she mad at me because I didn't support her in her extramarital dalliance? Who, in their right minds, would? Idiot.* She wondered whether she should call Aisha and ask her directly why she said what she did. Then, she decided not to because she wanted Aisha to apologise for saying such a thing. Siya was hurt that she had been cut off abruptly, even though she was doing it with Aisha's interest at heart. She decided to call Aisha after she had cooled down.

Have you thought of any possible themes for your next?

Manoj wanted to know via SMS. She replied saying that she would get back with some ideas shortly. Siya was busy trying to reply to Siddhant's message.

I'm so sorry to hear about your parents, Siddhant. It is difficult to see our loved ones suffer. But, why do you say that your dream of serving your country has not fructified? You're a soldier in the Army—isn't that what you always wanted, more than anything else? Does that not bring you immense joy? How many of us are fortunate enough to realise our dreams? Unless, it has not turned out to be what you hoped it would?

She had second thoughts, as always, but decided to send it before she could think anymore.

Signing out of Facebook, she logged into her email account and sent a list of titles to Manoj that she had been thinking of. Because her last topic had been serious, Siya mentioned in her email that she would like to write about the different kinds of friends one needs in one's life. Manoj asked her to go ahead with the idea. She embarked on her grocery shopping trip, thinking about her write-up and what to include; when she bumped into Ira in front of the elevator.

"Hi, Siya, how have you been? Haven't seen you in a while," said Ira, in the honeyed voice she used with Samar.

"Yeah, we've been travelling. Plus, I've been busy with work."

"Work? Have you taken up a job? Where?"

"With a social networking site. I'm a freelance writer with them."

"Oh...," said Ira, trying to hide her dismay, unsuccessfully. Siya wondered if she was disappointed that she actually had some talent besides being married to Samar!

As the elevator stopped on their floor, they entered it together. "Since you are freelancing, you would definitely have time to spare. Our first rehearsal for the Navaratri celebration is scheduled for this weekend. Come to the multipurpose room on Saturday at 11 am. I'm sure we could use you somewhere," she said, looking down at her, literally.

"But, Navaratri is months away! What's the hurry?" Siya asked in a small voice, remembering Imran's advice.

"I know. It takes time to sift through the people. We have to decide who are the good dancers and who are not. With most of us working through the week and sometimes weekends too, planning ahead is very important."

"Oh," Siya's face fell as the lifeline seemed to be slipping out of her hand. "I'm sorry I won't be able to participate," she blurted out, thinking hard for a good reason.

"Why?" Ira asked, unable to understand why Siya did not realise how lucky she was at being offered this chance!

"Because...because we are planning something big for the community and I will be required to execute it," Siya said with relief.

"What? A writing competition?" she asked, brimming with sarcasm.

Pulling herself straight, as tall as she could in her two-inch heels, Siya's head buzzed with what she could say to combat it. In a voice that was cool, calm and devoid of sarcasm, she said, "No, not a writing competition but a flash mob. It's all the rage these days. I'm sure you've seen plenty of videos online."

Ira's face lost a bit of colour…it seemed like someone had suddenly deflated this Amazonian woman. As the lift stopped on the ground floor, Siya walked out first, holding her head high, triumphantly, as she filed the priceless picture of Ira with her mouth agape in her mind forever!

As Siya did the rounds of the supermarket and exhibition galleries, her mind was preoccupied. She wondered why she had said that and how could she possibly organise a flash mob. But the expression on Ira's face was totally worth it!

29

Siya walked to the ATM to withdraw cash on her way back home. Her eyes were immediately drawn to the mannequin in the Nike window. She walked in, wondering if the leopard print top she had seen some time back was still available. She was overjoyed at being able to fit into a medium-sized top!

Feeling buoyed, Siya came back home and decided to work on the piece. She wished to dedicate it to Aisha. She was too happy at being rewarded for her efforts to lose weight to hold on to any anger towards her. Aisha's innocuous remark at their first meeting in the gallery had goaded her on this path of weight loss in earnest. Before that, she had dilly dallied with diets and exercise whenever it was convenient but of late, her approach to food had evolved. She wanted to go meet her and chat with her, just like they used to. Aisha had got Siya back into writing again. By the time her kids were home, she had written and edited her piece. Suitably satisfied, she sent it across to Manoj.

By evening, she received a reply from Manoj stating that he was happy with it and didn't think any changes were required. It would be published the next day.

Siya immediately sent a message to Aisha:

Hi! Hope you are feeling better now. Can I come to see you some time? I miss our conversations with chai…

She waited for an immediate reply but none came.

As luck would have it, Samar asked Siya later that evening, "How's your friend Aisha? She had hurt her back, *na*? Did you go to see her?"

Siya didn't know how to respond. She decided not to tell him everything. "She was in pain when I saw her last week. She was hopeful she would recover soon. In fact, I messaged her today only. Will let you know how she's feeling when I see her again."

Next morning, Siya woke up to a message from Aisha that put a smile on her face.

I've missed you too, Siya. I've behaved very badly with you; I'm sorry about that. It's just that I am emotionally overwrought right now. I would love to chat with you over chai/coffee, so please come soon!

S: *Super! Will message you before coming today.*

As soon as Siya returned from the gym, she logged into Facebook to check if her write up had been uploaded. It was. She messaged Aisha immediately that she would be there in an hour.

As was her habit of late, she clicked on the Messages icon on Facebook instinctively. There was a message from Siddhant. Siya inhaled deeply as she recalled what she had asked him in her last message. She braced herself to read the reply.

My life hasn't turned out the way I had expected it to. Why blame the Army alone? We seem to be at loggerheads all the time—my dreams and my reality. Having said that, I am so happy to have found you again that this time I won't let you go. Siya, I'm going to be in Mumbai next month. I want to meet you. Will let you know the exact dates as soon as my leave is approved.

On a separate note, do you believe in second chances? I know I do.

Siya was annoyed. *You didn't find me; I found you. Liar. Now, I'm wondering why? Why did I go looking for him?* She wondered if she still had feelings for him.

No way! She would definitely like to meet him...but, how would it be to meet someone from your past again? *What if I'm frozen, like that time when Amitabh Bachchan stood in front of me at the hotel? Second chances? I don't know... What the hell does he mean?* She was offended that he thought she was a desperate housewife looking for a fling... *How dare he even think on those lines. Idiot. Men are so full of themselves; just can't imagine that someone may not be attracted to them anymore. If you're not, then why are you entertaining him?*

Siya's phone buzzed just then. It was the driver calling to tell her that he had returned home. She remembered that she had to go meet Aisha. She immediately logged out of Facebook after quickly scanning the message one last time.

An hour later, Siya was standing outside Aisha's apartment, with a bunch of white roses in her hand. As soon as the door was opened, Siya rushed in towards the bedroom. She stopped in her tracks when she saw Aisha sitting on the sofa with her legs propped up. Aisha looked up and smiled at Siya. On the table next to her were scattered some books and CDs. She had taken Siya's advice, after all. She was dressed in shorts and a tee and looking better than she had last week.

"Aisha! It's so good to see you sitting up. You're obviously feeling better," she said, enveloping her in a warm hug.

"Yes, I am. No more pain, thankfully."

Handing her the bunch of white roses, Siya said, "I come in peace."

"O Siya, don't embarrass me. I'm the one who acted so childishly with you and the gym trainer. I'm sorry," she said, her eyes downcast.

"Aisha, don't overthink it. I was perplexed then but now I'm just so relieved we are talking again that I don't want to dwell on it."

"Great! You look slimmer every time I see you—how much more weight do you plan to lose?" Aisha asked Siya, in an effort to stay on a 'safe' topic.

"I still have two kilos to go…but it's becoming harder. We were away for the weekend with Samar's friend who is a psychologist."

"Oh, where did you go?" she asked.

"We went to Aamby Valley, just three hours away. It's a beautiful place. It's hard to believe that you are in India when you are there!"

"Really? That good? I've been looking for a nice getaway too. I will look it up. So, you were telling me about Samar's psycho friend!" They burst out laughing at that remark. "Before we get totally absorbed in our conversation, let me just ask for tea and coffee. Green, for you, I presume!" Siya nodded as Aisha pressed a small buzzer lying on the table. Her maid walked into the living room. "*Ek coffee aur ek green tea le aao*, please," she instructed.

Turning back to Siya, Aisha motioned for her to continue. "He informed me about some studies that have been conducted to prove that the negative feelings we harbour inside keep adding up, resulting in unhealthy weight gain. You know, sometimes we don't express what we want to truly say or do. In fact, we do the contrary. If we don't deal with such feelings or issues in time they settle on our bodies in the form of stubborn fat. The only way to lose it is to deal with it, head on," said Siya, sighing.

Aisha watched her in silence. "So, what's the problem? Sounds like detox to me—inside and out."

"The problem is...that there are so many issues. How does one put a finger on it? How do I know which one will free the stubborn fat up, making it melt and disappear? Some of them have their genesis in my childhood, some in my youth and some are ongoing. People cannot just change overnight," Siya confessed.

"He didn't say anything about changing people. It's about closure. Do you have unresolved issues?" Aisha asked, gently. *Do I?* Siya thought, her gaze fixed inwardly, at a point in the past. *Am I seeking closure?* When Siya didn't say anything, Aisha continued, "We all do...we tend to brush serious things under the carpet instead of taking them head on, hoping that they'll disappear just because we can't see them. But, they lie buried deep within like a thorn that gets under your skin, bleeding you dry without hurting you on the outside." Aisha paused. She had a faraway look in her eyes, as if she too had travelled to another place, another time. She slowly turned to look at Siya with sorrowful eyes. "That is why I reconnected with Manav. After years of bleeding silently...thoughts of him wouldn't go away. Even though I married Neel, became domesticated, had children... I could not comprehend why he didn't want me as much." Siya inhaled sharply, reaching out to hold her hand. *Is that the reason I reconnected with Siddhant? Do I want to know, at a subconscious level, why he didn't want me anymore? Was I not good? Was I not enough?*

"Manav was very penitent when I wrote to him. He said he had asked my friends and acquaintances about me when he realised how foolish he had been to let me go. They told him that I was married in the US. A couple of months later, he contacted me through Facebook. We struck up a conversation. One conversation led to another till I was so consumed with the desire to see him in person that I went into depression. Neel assumed that moving back to India would help me. I jumped at the chance. It was almost as if the Universe was making this happen for me!"

Aisha looked at Siya pointedly, holding her gaze. "Don't judge me, Siya, but I think I finally have a chance at love. Manav is my one true love. I've always loved only him."

But, what about Neel, Aisha? He truly loves you. And, what about your kids? Have you thought of them? Siya didn't voice her thoughts out loud; she couldn't. "So, what's your plan now?" she asked instead.

"Well, we have gotten really close during my trips to Delhi recently. He says he loves me too. I've decided to pop the question to him—we've wasted enough time already! I can't wait to start spending my life with him," she enthused.

Siya smiled feebly. "I'm sorry I don't know what to say… I've never had a friend in this situation before," she explained.

"Never mind. I don't expect you to say anything…in fact, it's best if you don't. It's such a relief to be able to share this with you though. I've been keeping all of this to myself for so long that I was getting antsy. You tell me. What's new with you?" she asked, smiling brightly at Siya, as she sipped on her coffee.

Should I or shouldn't I? Siya debated with herself. *I think she has enough on her plate right now; let me not burden her with my issues too. I will tell her later.*

"Oh, I almost forgot!" Siya exclaimed, as she got up to fetch her laptop from the table. Opening it, she logged into Facebook and brought up the article that Manoj had uploaded and placed it on Aisha's lap. Siya sipped her tea as Aisha read the piece. "Nicely done, Siya! So, which one of these 'type' of friends am I?" she asked.

"You are a little bit of every type. I've known you for long, there are things I can definitely learn from you, we have a lot in common and last but not the least, you are my go-to friend!"

Aisha grinned. "As you are mine," she said, solemnly. "Oh, did I tell you? Manoj called me last evening. He was really praising you. He said how self-driven you are; always thinking of different topics to write on, events that you could cover etc. He was telling me how people in the community have gotten together to seriously re-work some laws concerning children in television today, all thanks to your article."

"I'm happy that people took it so seriously. I really feel strongly about the way children are being deprived of a normal childhood. What else did he say? Anything about paying me pot loads of money?" Siya asked, laughing out loud.

"No money talk. It's a start-up, remember? But, he did say how he'd like to target the younger demographic of this community, bring them together as a voice in a language they understand. He just didn't know how..." her voice trailed off.

"Flash mob!" Siya exclaimed, her voice filled with wonder at her own idea.

"What? What did you say?" Aisha asked.

"Flash mob," Siya repeated.

"Flash mob? That's a great idea, Siya! And, its' so cool too. He'll love it. Call and tell him right now," Aisha said, her voice rising with excitement.

"You think he'll buy it? Really?" Siya asked, hesitating as she picked up her cell phone.

"Trust me. Just call him," Aisha reassured her.

Sure enough, Manoj was thrilled with the idea and couldn't wait to get started. He said he would post it online, calling all youngsters (and the not-so-young too!) to come forward and participate. They could look at doing it on Independence Day! Once he had a fair number of participants, he would call for a meeting wherein they could discuss details. He couldn't stop thanking Siya for such a well-timed idea. Siya grinned at Aisha as she ended the call. "Didn't I say he would be totally sold?" she asked.

"Yeah. He kept thanking me; it became embarrassing after a while," Siya remarked.

"Now is the time to ask for that pot of money!" Aisha joked. "Maybe you should wait till the flash mob happens. It'll be all over social media, especially since there are youngsters participating. I hope you're going to be in it too," Aisha asked Siya pointedly.

"Me? I don't know a thing about dancing. Besides, I can't remember a routine of steps...it's mind boggling for me," Siya replied.

"Don't be silly. You'll get enough time to practice. Besides, you're doing it for fun; it's not a contest. Just follow the people around you if you get confused or lost; you'll be fine," Aisha placated her.

"Will you participate, Aisha? It'll be good to have you beside me," Siya asked.

"I would have really liked to but I don't want to risk anything with my back. I want it to heal as quickly as possible so I can travel to Delhi. I've waited too long to start living my life on my terms. But, I'll definitely come to cheer for you!" she said, giving her a warm hug.

"Aisha, please don't get me wrong—I hope you are able to find the peace and happiness that has been eluding you. Let me know when you leave for Delhi," she said, taking Aisha's hands in her own. "I'll be in touch."

Delhi, August 1994

I want to break free—Queen

I wrote him a letter later that day. It took me a while to string the words together. I didn't want to sound needy or lovesick. However, it had been a traumatic experience for me. I was mad at him for having put me through that hell. I wanted to see his reaction.

"That which I was dreading, finally happened. I got pregnant. I reckon it happened the day we were in your friend's hostel room… I should have been firm with you.

It's been very nerve wracking and scary for me. I don't know what I would have done or how I would have managed if my Didi had not been there. I will never forgive you for putting me in this situation. I could have…anything could have happened to me. I think it's best we don't meet anymore."

I deliberately kept it devoid of any endearments and to the point.

It generally took 4–5 days for a letter to reach him. In the meanwhile, I thought about what I finally wanted. He called later that week. It was around 7:30 pm. Coincidentally, I answered the landline. "Hi. I got your letter today. How are you now?" No endearments from him. No apology either. It cut like a knife.

I was very aloof and monosyllabic. "I'm fine." No apology still.

The conversation was filled with pregnant pauses, neither one of us acknowledging the elephant in the room. "I'm going to be in Delhi soon. I will call you." No apology.

"I have already told you—I don't think we should meet or write."

"But, I have some things of yours that I need to return... can't we meet once?" Still, no apology.

"You can keep them. I don't need them anymore." And, I hung up.

From that day on, I waited. I waited without knowing I was waiting. For a phone call or a chance meeting...hoping that he would turn up suddenly to surprise me. I imagined that he would apologise profusely and beg forgiveness. He would tell me that he couldn't live without me or my letters, he would proclaim that we were meant to be together forever, he would solemnly swear that he had meant it when he had said he wanted us to grow old together....

30

The wheels were set in motion as soon as Manoj posted news of the flash mob online. He called her one evening, two days after the post. "Siya, entries are pouring in like the Mumbai rain! I had no idea people would be so enthused."

Siya laughed. "Isn't that a good sign?" she asked.

"Of course! I will have to set a deadline for entries though. So many other details need to be finalised. I've never organised anything like this before—I have to educate myself first!"

Siya was delighted at the excitement in his voice. "Don't worry, Manoj, we'll figure it out. Let's make a list of things that need to be done," she prompted.

"Hmmm, first and foremost, we have to appoint a choreographer who can teach everyone. We have to be clear that no money will be offered as it's a collaborative effort."

"Got it. Let me ask amongst the people I know if they can recommend someone. Next?" Siya asked.

"Secondly, a song, preferably something that youngsters are listening to, has to be chosen."

"Of course! Let's have an introductory meeting with the participants once you close entries. I'm sure most answers will come up then."

"Good idea, Siya. Will decide on a date and share with you. I just hope rain doesn't play havoc with our plans."

Siya had not shared this latest development with Samar; she wanted it to be a surprise. Manoj called for a meeting the following Saturday at 4 pm. *Shucks, why does he want to meet on a Saturday? What if Samar and the kids want to plan something?* She had to think of a plausible excuse to get out of the house on a weekend by herself.

"Are we doing anything tomorrow?" she asked Samar at the dinner table on Friday night. Samar said that there were no plans as such. "Cool. I want to try out a new workout called spinning—it's all the rage these days. I believe Bollywood celebrities are queuing up for it. I'll sign up for a trial class at four pm tomorrow," she suggested, watching Samar closely for a reaction.

"Sure" he said, suitably impressed at her zeal for workouts and losing weight.

Come Saturday, Siya was surprised at the number of people who showed up for the meeting. "Boy! I didn't think so many would turn up," she exclaimed to Manoj.

"The power of social media," he answered. Once preliminary introductions were made, Manoj threw the floor open to song suggestions until a consensus was reached on the song. It was to be 'Gangnam Style'. A choreographer was appointed from a bunch of college kids. Lastly, rehearsal days and timings had to be fixed. This was the most challenging aspect of the effort since the mob comprised of students, working professionals, and homemakers. While the homemakers preferred weekday mornings (when kids were away in school) for practice sessions, students preferred weekday evenings as they had classes to attend in the mornings. Working professionals, on the other hand, could only spare time on the weekends for practice. It was maddening!

As Siya plunged into dance rehearsals, Aisha was focusing on the road to recovery. While Siya was juggling time between her home, kids, and the community; Aisha had enrolled into a week-long ayurvedic treatment to expedite the healing process.

News about the impending flash mob spread like fire in the small, tech savvy community of Powai. More and more people joined in as rehearsals picked up pace. Siya was very self-conscious at these rehearsals. *Gosh, they move so fluidly!* she thought one evening as she watched sixteen-year-old girls showing them the steps. Most of them were students of the Shiamak Davar Dance Academy that had become so popular recently. Siya met a lot of new people during rehearsals. Most of them were moms, like her. Despite their age and weight, they danced beautifully, while Siya stumbled through the steps, desperately trying to memorise the sequence.

Siya had not been able to get Siddhant's message out of her mind. Though she hadn't replied to it yet, she constantly thought about it. She asked herself many questions but the answers always eluded her. The thought of meeting him was so exciting! She couldn't wait to see how he would react when he saw her again, after so many years. She wondered if he would still find her attractive. She did not look very different, except for the weight she had put on. Thankfully, she had managed to lose quite a bit of it.

She wanted to meet him. She needed answers. She sent him a reply and decided to tell Samar too.

Did I tell you that I am going to be part of a flash mob? I'm really looking forward to it! We've been practising our routine for many days now. Watch out for it!

The thought of seeing you again after all these years is a bit surreal... Do let me know your exact dates so I can tell you what suits me.

Walking back home from the dance rehearsal one evening, Siya bumped into the Deadly Divas. Taking in her sweat-drenched workout gear and flushed face, they couldn't resist asking if she was coming from the gym. "No, not exactly. I'm coming from a dance practice."

"Dance? Really? Where do you go to learn? Shiamak Davar?" Naina asked, curiosity getting the better of her.

"Actually, we are putting together a flash mob."

"A flash mob! Where? When? I'd like to sign up too!" Naina squealed in delight.

"Are you not part of the Powai community online?" Siya asked, looking at Ira who was rolling her eyes at them.

"No! What's that all about? Tell me *na*, I'm really keen to join," Naina pleaded.

Wow! She wants to be part of something I'm doing! "It's an online group...you can join it on Facebook. But, I'm not sure if we are taking any more people since we already have over thirty dancers. I can check with Manoj if you are keen, he's the one who is leading this initiative," she answered with pride in her voice.

"Please do. We both would love to!" she said, clutching her arm as if she wouldn't let go till she said yes.

"Really?" Siya asked, directing her gaze at Ira, waiting for her to make a request.

As Naina and Siya waited, Ira looked flustered. "It's too much of a commitment, babe. There will be rehearsals to attend... I don't have the time or bandwidth to deal with it right now," Ira answered, despairingly.

"We'll manage, doll." Siya looked away so they wouldn't see her roll her eyes. *Doll? Really?* "We'll go for one rehearsal to see the steps and then we can practice on our own. I'll help you. Let's go, please," she pleaded with Ira.

At Naina's insistence, Ira caved in. Smiling through gritted teeth at Siya, she said, "Okay," as Naina let out a yelp of victory.

"Please let us know if we can participate after speaking with your friend," Naina reminded Siya.

"Sure. I will," said Siya, walking away towards the lift, a smile plastered on her face.

"Guess who wants to be part of the surprise I mentioned to you earlier?" she asked Samar, as they were finishing dinner that evening.

"Who?" he asked.

"Take a guess," she teased.

"That's not fair! I don't have any idea what the surprise is; how can I guess?" he asked, trying to look cross.

Siya smiled, unsure if he should tell him. "Okay, if you guess it right then I will tell you what the surprise is," she answered, trying to placate him.

"Cool. Give me a hint on the person then," he said.

"Mmmm...someone who dislikes me as much as she likes you!" she answered, her eyes twinkling.

"Aah...our neighbour!" he answered, confidently.

"Bingo! Can you believe it? Naina and she want to be part of something I'm associated with!"

Samar grinned, prompting her to share the surprise. "So, what do they want to be a part of?"

"A flashmob!" she said with a stupid grin.

"A flashmob. Wow! That sounds like fun. I would have never thought Manoj could come up with that!"

"Actually, it was my idea…in a desperate attempt to get away from the Navaratri celebration," she said, pretending to wipe the sweat off her forehead.

"Great! So, what did you tell them?"

"I said I'd check with Manoj. We already have a lot of participants, I don't know if he wants to bring in new people since we are just weeks away."

"Has the date been finalised? When is it?" he asked.

"15th August."

"Ah, there's not much time left then. But, who knows? They may be good at picking up steps and integrating with the group, no?" Siya was irked that Samar was canvassing for them, but she decided not to react.

"Yeah, who knows. I'll talk to Manoj," she said.

Siya joined him on the sofa later that night after tucking the boys in. She looked at Samar who was engrossed with the news item on TV. "Samar, remember I told you about my friend from college who has been helping me with my articles?"

"Mmmm…" he answered, nodding absently.

"He's coming into town and I am planning to meet him."

"Oh, really? Ok…he's in the Army, *na*?" he asked, his gaze fixed on the TV.

Siya was taken aback. *So, he did pay attention when I mentioned this the last time. Men are not so disinterested after all!* "You know, I would have enrolled in the Army if I hadn't got admission in a college of my choice. That was my Plan B," he said, turning around to face her. "But then, I wouldn't have met you. And, we wouldn't be together today. So, I'm glad I didn't need to use Plan B!" he said, surprising her with a kiss. "Are you calling him home?" he asked.

"NO!" she exclaimed rather vehemently. "I mean, I don't know where he'll be staying. If he's in South Mumbai then it could be a long way off—better to meet mid-way, I thought," she said, regaining her composure.

"That makes sense," he said, turning back to the news.

Phew! Thank goodness, she thought.

31

Siya, I can't believe how you have changed since we started corresponding. I remember initially how you were frustrated; trying to figure out what you could do with your free time. You were searching for answers... Today, you are writing about things close to your heart and being socially responsible. I'm really looking forward to meeting you again. I could do with some of your enthusiasm!

A smiled played on Siya's lips as she read Siddhant's message the next day. *It's true that I have changed in the last couple of months. Do I owe some of it to him? Has talking to him boosted my confidence? Or, is it because I have found my calling through writing? With purpose comes a sense of self-worth. Thank God, I have finally found mine.*

The same day Siya received a text message from Aisha.

Going to Delhi for the long weekend in August—tickets booked! I'm so sorry I will miss your flash mob dance. I'm sure you will rock it! Wish me luck.

Siya smiled. And then she realised why Aisha was so excited...she pursed her lips. *Why do I feel anxious? I'm planning on doing the same... You are just meeting him, Siya; not planning on leaving your husband and kids. That's true... I hope she doesn't do anything stupid. I hope he treats her well.*

She replied:

I hope you recover fully soon, Aisha. Have fun in Delhi! May love and luck accompany you wherever you go. Will talk to you before that.

That evening, after rehearsal, Manoj requested everyone to stay back to finalise some details. Although Manoj was not part of the dancers, he would always be present when practice sessions were on. He had emptied a large space on the ground floor of his bungalow for them to rehearse. "Everybody, I need your suggestions on the possible venues we can have the flash mob. It should be a prominently visible spot with high footfalls, else we will not be able to attract people in large numbers," he announced as loudly as he possibly could.

Various suggestions were made—Heritage Park, Forest Club, Haiko Circle, the Powai lakefront, the space outside Aromas Café... They started debating on the pros and cons of each location, settling for the circle at Aromas Café. "Let me start working on procuring the required permits. Since this is a public space, it may cause some traffic congestion or chaos otherwise. Also, some element of security would be required to ensure the dancers pull it off without any hassles. If anyone here has any contacts with the local police or administration, please step forward and pitch in. The others need to start praying to the Rain gods so they don't dampen our plans. We don't have much time left...," he concluded.

As the crowd dispersed, Siya approached Manoj. "Manoj, can I talk to you for a moment?"

"Of course, Siya."

"I wanted to ask if we are still taking on more people. Some of my neighbours are interested in joining."

"Are they good friends of yours?" he asked.

Siya was taken aback. "Not really…" her voice trailed off.

"Then, we can't include them at this stage," he declared with finality. Siya fell silent. "Is that okay, Siya?" he asked, his tone softening. She looked at him and smiled sheepishly. "Siya, we have only two weeks to go for the flash mob. Any new people joining in at this stage will have to be very good dancers, who can not only pick up the steps quickly but also merge with the rest seamlessly. Do you think your neighbours can do that?" he asked.

Siya thought about it. She had to admit that both of them were naturally gifted dancers and would fit right in. It was a tough call. "Yes! Yes, I've seen them dance. I think they'll merge beautifully," Siya declared in a rush, afraid she had lost Manoj's attention.

"If you are confident, then please go ahead and bring them along. I trust you," Manoj said.

Siya always walked back home from the rehearsal. It was a short walk during which she generally went over the steps repeatedly so they would be imprinted on her brain. However, on this particular evening, she was wondering how she would approach the Divas to share the news. *Should I tell Naina or Ira? Definitely Naina…she was more excited. If I chance upon them in the lobby then I will tell them there itself, else, I'll go to Naina's house.*

As luck would have it, the Divas were not around the porch or lobby. *I'll just have to go to her house…hmmmpphh.* Siya took the flight of stairs up to the second floor and rang the bell. Shifting the weight of her gym bag from one shoulder to the other, she waited patiently. The door was opened after what seemed like a long time by Naina. "Oh, hi! How are you Siya?" she asked, her voice devoid of the enthusiasm that was such an intrinsic part of her personality.

"I'm good. Listen, I stopped by just to tell you that I spoke with Manoj about you guys joining in the flash mob."

"Oh…and, what did he say?" she asked, her interest suddenly piqued.

"He said that he wouldn't take new people on at such an advanced stage because you would have to pick up the steps really fast and integrate with the group."

"Oh, we can pick up steps in a day," she commented, nonchalantly.

Siya's eyes widened at her self-confidence. "I know. That's what I told him. So, you guys can come for rehearsal tomorrow," she said.

Naina's eyes widened. "What? Really? You told him that we could do it? That is so nice of you…," she said, beaming at Siya, as she grabbed her hands.

"Ira!" she yelled, turning around. "Come here…fast." *Oh, Ira is here too—good!* "Come inside, Siya," Naina said, in the most dulcet tone possible.

"No, it's okay, I have to get home. It's play-time for the kids. I like to be around in the park," she stopped mid-sentence when she saw Ira. Her eyes were swollen, her makeup askew. She was walking towards the door but her eyes were elsewhere. Naina turned around and excitedly shared the news that Siya had brought with her. She smiled feebly.

"That's nice," she commented, in a matter-of-fact tone.

"Great! So, I'll see you ladies tomorrow. I'll message you the address now," she said to Naina. "Bye then," she waved at the duo as she turned around to walk towards the lift.

"Wait. I'm coming too," she heard Ira's voice call from behind.

"Are you sure, doll?" Naina asked, facing her.

"Yes, I'm fine now. I'll be okay," she said, giving her a hug. "I'll see you tomorrow," she said, giving her a quick peck on the cheek. "Okay!" As the lift stopped, Siya walked in first. She quickly stole a glance at Ira in the mirror. She looked pale...and sad. She pressed the button to their floor and stood to one side, quietly. Surreptitiously, Siya glanced at her face again. She wanted to ask if everything was okay but she was so accustomed to being rebuffed by her that she didn't dare. Ira, on the other hand, made no attempt at conversation. As the lift stopped on their floor, they walked in opposite directions, towards their homes, in silence.

"Take care, Ira," Siya called out loudly. Ira turned around. She nodded at Siya with a blank expression.

"I will, thanks," she said. Inhaling deeply, she opened the door to her apartment and walked in.

"You'll be happy to know that the Divas are coming to audition for the flash mob." Siya informed Samar, as she keenly observed his face for a reaction, later that evening.

"That's good! I'm sure they'll ace it," he said, smugly. Siya was stumped. *He has so much confidence in them!* Before she could voice her thoughts with sarcasm, he remarked, "I'm glad you didn't let your insecurities get the better of you." *He is more astute than I give him credit for!* "What? What's the matter? Why are you smiling?" he asked, catching her smile.

"I'm just surprised at how astute you have become. I would have never thought..."

"Siya, I know how your mind works. You tend to mull over things excessively, weighing pros and cons, trying to resolve issues rationally but ultimately your conscience is your best guide."

Siya didn't know how to respond. "I am really surprised," she said when she finally found her voice.

"And, you think I pay no attention," Samar retorted, with a twinkle in his eyes.

"Ever since I have lost weight, you do," she said, teasing him.

"That's not true," he protested, but she silenced him with a kiss.

"That reminds me... Ira didn't seem to be herself today. She looked like she had been crying. Something was not right," Siya said, as Samar broke away from the embrace.

"Hmmm," said Samar, absentmindedly. "Did you ask her?"

"No, I wasn't sure she'd want to tell me. I just told her to take care."

"Great!"

"Any news of Imran and Maya?" she asked.

"Yeah. I spoke with Imran. They will be visiting his parents next month."

"Oh, that's nice. I haven't spoken with Maya since Aamby. Let me message her to get together some time before they go."

Picking up her phone, she sent a message to Maya asking her whether she would be free to meet soon.

32

The next morning, she received a message from Maya.

Today looks difficult. How about tomorrow? Around 4 pm. Does that work for you?

Siya: *The kids are back by then. Why don't you come home?*

Maya: *I'd love to meet your boys again! Will see you at 4 pm tomorrow. Please share your address.*

Smiling at that, Siya messaged her again: *1902, Solitaire. Looking forward!*

The next day, Siya made the boys change out of their uniforms as soon as they got back from school. She generally let them hang around in it for a while as they played with their toys or watched a favourite cartoon show on TV. After six hours of being told what to do and what not to do, she figured they needed a break. Since she was expecting Maya, she wanted to make a good impression with her kids. "Wash your face and hands well. Take off your shoes and socks, put them away in the shoe cupboard," she fired instructions one after the other.

"Why, Mama? Why can't I change later?" Aryan asked.

"Because Mama has a friend coming over. Remember Maya Aunty who came to Aamby with us? I want her to see my boys looking fresh and tidy," she explained.

"Your friend is coming. You should look fresh and tidy. Why us?" Arjun asked, innocently.

Taking him in her arms, Siya said, "So she can see your cute face and charming smile and tell me what handsome boys I have! Don't you want to be complimented?"

"What's compli…that difficult word you used?" he asked. As she answered his question, she carried him into the bathroom to wash up and change.

The intercom buzzed at 4 pm. "Hello. *Maya memsaab aayee hai,*" the security guard announced when Siya answered the phone. Siya smiled. *Maya Memsaab indeed…except this one is so different from the fictional character. She lives under no false illusion, she loves the man she has married without the shadow of a doubt. Maya Memsaab was continuously searching for a love that eluded her…like Aisha.*

The chiming of the doorbell interrupted her train of thoughts. Maya walked in, looking stunning in a white Lucknowi salwar kameez. "Come, let's sit," Siya said, ushering her into the drawing room.

"What a lovely home you have, Siya! Let me see how you have done it up," she said, as her eyes took in the wicker *jhoola,* trendy wooden furniture with a touch of ethnicity, feature walls in shades of amber and scarlet. "Modern and traditional side by side—how nice," Maya exclaimed. Walking towards the dining room, she squealed in delight as her eyes alighted on the Movie Wall. It was painted in bright yellow—the colour of a ripe mango, and had framed posters of movies from Hollywood and Bollywood adorning it. A studio light stood in one corner of the room, complementing the theme. "Wow! I love this. As would Imran…has he seen this yet? I didn't know you are such a movie freak!"

Siya beamed. "We both enjoy movies, grew up on a steady diet of films which we remember fondly even today."

"This is so quirky and fun!"

Just then, Aryan and Arjun trooped into the living room. Surprisingly, they ran up to Maya and hugged her. She was so overwhelmed at their innocent expression of love that her eyes moistened immediately. "It's been so long since my kids ran up to me and hugged me like this. The best therapy in the world, if you ask me," she said, bringing out two boxes of chocolates, one for each of them. Squealing with delight, the boys jumped and ran into the kitchen to show their gifts to Vaishali Didi.

"That's so true! What will you drink, Maya? Adrak wali chai or filter coffee?" Siya asked, steering the conversation in another direction.

"Both sound tempting! I think I'll go with the filter coffee; it's been a long time since I had that!" As they sat in the living room overlooking the Powai Lake, the clouds gathered slowly overhead. "It looks like it's just going to rain," Maya commented.

"Yup. This is your first time experiencing the famous Mumbai monsoon," Siya remarked, "how is it going?" They discussed various aspects of the rainy season including Do's and Don'ts. The conversation then turned to what each of them was doing.

Siya told Maya about her conversation with Imran at Aamby. "Really? I didn't know Imran and you discussed your weight loss program. What did he have to say?"

"He said that negative feelings and emotions deposit themselves on one's body in the form of unhealthy fat. In order to lose the fat, it is important to let go of issues that affect you deeply. I'm trying to figure out what those are for now…," said Siya, in a pensive voice.

"That sounds like something Imran would say. Have you made any headway with that? I know it's a very personal matter and I don't want to intrude but, if I can help in any way please let me know," said Maya.

Smiling wryly, Siya said, "I haven't really dwelt on it much. I'm pre-occupied with thoughts of my friend, Aisha. She is going through some stuff…and planning to take drastic steps that could throw her life in a tizzy. I have tried to warn her but not emphatically enough as I'm afraid I may lose her friendship…"

"Being a good friend is not easy…sometimes, you have to do what's right rather than what's easy…your conscience needs to be clear. I can't live with a prickly conscience, I can live with one less friend," Maya said, in an empathetic tone.

I don't want to live without Aisha, I've only just found her! But, Siya didn't voice it.

Siya was glad she could use Maya as a sounding board in such times. She wondered aloud, how Maya turned out to be so wise.

"You live and learn! I've been through some shit in my life but thankfully, nothing scarred me permanently. Imran has been such a blessing. I can say anything or do anything; he doesn't judge me. He lets me learn from my mistakes. That's the best thing about him," Maya said, her eyes shining with love.

"You mean, it's not important to you that he is drop dead gorgeous!" exclaimed Siya.

Maya laughed out loud. "Of course, darling, that's why I let him treat me in the first place," she said, winking.

"So, how's your ex-boyfriend doing?" Maya asked as Vaishali placed a tray with tea, coffee and biscuits on the centre table. Siya's face froze. *Did Vaishali hear that? Would she have understood?* Stealing a look at Vaishali, she tried to gauge her reaction even as she walked away nonchalantly. Sensing her discomfort, Maya said, "But we don't have to talk about men all the time. Tell me something new," she insisted.

Siya told her about the flash mob, earning her approval right away. "Look at me, only talking about myself. That's being a bad hostess... What have you been doing, Maya?" Siya asked with genuine interest.

"I've been meeting some very interesting people, mostly artists, of late. I've been toying with the idea of an Art camp away from the city. Since you are so tuned in to the community, do you think people would be interested?"

"Of course! I think it's a great idea. I'm sure people would be interested. We could conduct a survey to find out."

"A survey? Really?"

"Yes. Just to figure out what sort of art form people are interested in—visual or performing. Are you looking at a residential camp or a day-long workshop?" Siya asked.

"Well, I haven't thought about it in such detail but what you are saying makes sense. A survey would throw up answers and then we could design the program accordingly. Music, painting, yoga could all be woven into the structure."

"That sounds like fun! Let me talk to Manoj once this flash mob is over. Till then, why don't you give it some more thought?" Siya urged.

The conversation continued, meandering from one topic to the other with ease. Maya gathered her handbag as the clouds started to loom threateningly over the lake. "I better get home before the downpour starts! Don't want to get stuck in a jam. Imran is always worried about that," Maya said, apologising for breaking up their tete-a-tete.

"Don't be silly, Maya, I wouldn't want you to get stuck either. By the way, I will be meeting him soon," Siya blurted, like a teenager.

Maya was perplexed. As understanding dawned, Maya asked, "How come?"

It was Siya's turn to be confused. "Did you not suggest an ego massage?"

"Yes, I did. But, I thought he lives in another city."

"He'll be visiting soon."

"Oh...that's fortuitous! So, tell me—have you asked yourself why you really want to meet him?" Siya nodded her head in negation. "Please do. Doctor's orders," she said, getting up to hug Siya.

Siya called Vaishali to check where the boys were, worried that they would get drenched. Luckily, they were playing safely in the building lobby. Samar was going to attend an official dinner straight from office. Siya was going to be all alone for a while. Maya's question had left Siya pensive. She sat on the *jhoola*, swinging it gently. Too many thoughts churned inside her head mirroring the dark clouds threatening outside. Mesmerised by the flashes of lightning, she kept asking herself why she really wanted to meet Siddhant.

On the one hand, she wanted to see him. Really see him. *It will be like travelling back in time.* Just the sight of his face on Facebook was enough to make her yearn for a time that's gone forever. *That's normal, right? People visit places where they've grown up and schools they had good times in...because of the memories they associate with them.* Was that the only reason she wanted to meet him? She wondered. If truth be told, she wanted *him* to see *her*. She wanted him to see what he didn't have...what he could have had. Everybody was complimenting her on how much weight she'd lost. She knew she was looking good. He needed to see her like this. She should be one of his biggest regrets. She had a loving husband, beautiful home and adorable kids. And, he? He was by himself, all alone, shuttling from place to place with no sense of belonging, no roots anywhere. He had no one to come home to. *It must be an empty, lonely life.* He had said he wanted them to grow old together but he never showed up. He didn't even want to see how she was doing...that's what she wanted to ask him most of all—why didn't he show up? Why did he just disappear? She would have waited for him, if only he had asked her to.

There was a loud crackling of thunder as the clouds burst open forcefully. Rain. The swing stopped abruptly as the tears started streaming down her face. She needed answers; she wanted closure.

33

The next evening, Ira and Naina accompanied Siya to the dance rehearsal. She introduced them to Manoj as her friends and he asked her to take over. "Why don't you take them over to Prabha who can show them the steps?" he said. Turning to face them, he said, "Ladies, Siya has great faith in your ability to pick up the steps and gel with the group. Let's hope you prove her right! I'll see you around," he said, walking away to deal with other issues. Naina and Ira eyed Siya, a strange smile flitting on their faces—was it relief, gratitude or just appreciation?

"Come, let me introduce you to our choreographer, Prabha," said Siya, ushering them towards a heavy-set woman, dressed in slacks and a t-shirt. Naina and Ira exchanged looks of disbelief and a smirk. Siya caught the look just in time. "Just wait till you see her move," she said.

"Hey, Prabha! These are my friends who want to join in the flash mob. Can you please show them the steps once?" said Siya as she approached Prabha and gave her a hug.

"Siya, you don't need me to do that. You can do it!"

"No, no, Prabha; I still need practice. I don't want them messing up because of me. Please show them once; then I can practice the routine with them."

"You know what your problem is, Siya? You underestimate yourself. Come, we'll show them together," she said, pulling her alongside. She played the song on her phone, giving her the cue to follow. As soon as the music started, Prabha began dancing. Siya followed her closely, counting steps, all the while. She tried not to make eye contact with Naina or Ira—*that will definitely make me nervous.* At one point during the choreography, Siya was so mesmerised by the fluidity of Prabha's moves that she forgot to move herself! Laughing as she scampered to catch up, Siya joined in just as the music was drawing to a close. As the music ended with a flourish, Prabha and Siya froze in a stance for a few seconds and before breaking they high fived each other.

Naina and Ira burst into applause almost simultaneously. Surprised, Siya and Prabha turned around to face them, bowing in acknowledgment. "Fabulous! You are an amazing dancer, Prabha," Naina gushed.

"Isn't she? I just love the way she moves on the floor... so much grace," said Siya, chipping in happily.

"You were not bad yourself," said Naina, smiling sweetly.

"I'm not a dancer. I have two left feet. It's an effort for me to remember the sequence of steps. But, being part of a group that exudes such positive energy is worth going through this!"

"Hahaha! Does that mean you'll be okay if I don't put you in the first few rows?" Prabha asked, earnestly.

"Sweety, I'm okay even if you put me in the last row! As long as you don't relegate me to 'admin' work, I'm okay with any position," she said, beaming. As she turned around to face Naina and Ira, she caught them exchange a glance... was it discomfort or embarrassment?

"There you have it, ladies—the steps to follow and learn. Please don't waste any time. I can be a hard taskmaster," announced Prabha, in her booming voice. Naina and Ira quickly put their bags on the floor and ran up to Siya. They wanted to practice with her before the group got together to rehearse. At the end of one hour, they had gone over the routine a couple of times. They were naturally agile and had a keen sense of music, which helped them learn the moves in no time. Siya was really impressed.

When the group got together to rehearse, they fit in so seamlessly that it was hard to believe it was their first day. Even Manoj was thrilled! "Great work, ladies!" he said as he approached them at the end of the session. "Siya was right about your dancing skills. Though we would like more people to participate in this community effort, we have to be conscious of putting up a good show. I think the spectators are going to love it! There will be cries for Encore," he said, shaking hands as he moved on to the next group of participants, leaving the three of them beaming.

Walking back home together, they chatted some more about the song and their dance moves. Since dancing didn't come naturally to Siya, she always struggled with some steps. Naina and Ira showed her some tricks wherein she could use the natural movement of her body without agonising over perfection.

"I didn't know dancing was so scientific. I only use it to express gay abandon!" Siya justified in a lame voice.

"Hahaha!" They laughed in unison.

"That's precisely what dancing is meant to be—an expression of joy. Don't get bogged down by the dynamics of it. Just enjoy yourself when you dance, that is key," said Ira, smiling at her, leaving Siya stumped.

As they entered the building lobby, Naina turned to Siya and said, "Thank you for talking to Manoj and letting us in on the group. We appreciate it."

"You are both such fabulous dancers, it would have been unfair to keep you out of it," said Siya as they smiled on.

"We will see you day after at the rehearsal," said Ira, walking up the stairs with Naina to her apartment on the first floor.

34

On Thursday morning, Siya received a text message from Aisha.

Are you free to meet today? I'm a little nervous about my Delhi trip...

Siya pursed her lips as she read it.

Sure. Where and when?

Aisha: *Does 4 pm at Aromas suit you?*

Siya: *Yes. See you then!*

Siya settled the kids in with a snack on their return from school that afternoon before she headed out to Aromas. As she walked down the street, she counted the number of salons along the way. *Four salons within a radius of five hundred metres!* thought Siya, taking a seat inside the café. Looking around, she glanced at the people occupying other tables. There was a bunch of young girls, teenagers by the looks of it, preening into their phones as they took pictures of themselves.

We human beings are becoming more and more obsessed with how we look. But, how can we escape it? There's so much talk about flawless fair complexion, trendy clothes, the right accessories, ideal weight, healthy eats, diet plans, lustrous hair, anti-ageing...we are constantly being shown pictures of yummy mummies and perfect looking people in magazines, newspapers, television, social media. They make it so difficult for you to accept yourself as you are. I guess it's never been all about looks for me. If it was not for Aisha's offhand remark months ago, I would have blissfully continued to weigh sixty-five kilos (maybe more), happy with my minimal exercise routine and eating habits. I would have continued to envy those with great figures, labelling them as narcissistic. Truth be told, I've never pushed myself—didn't pursue a postgrad after college, gave up the MBA I enrolled in after Aryan was born… I've just been happy to be a homebody, not looking inwards or outwards.

If I'd not set out on this weight loss journey myself, I would have never realised how difficult it is to have an hour-glass figure! It's so much easier to go with the flow but then there's no personal growth. Isn't that ultimately what we should all aim for? Losing weight has made me feel good about myself, which has in turn led me to try new things. I would have run away from the thought of dancing in a public space six months ago but here I am—overcoming inhibitions! I have managed to accomplish what seemed insurmountable at the beginning, only through perseverance. So, losing weight is not only about being slim; it helps you to discover the reserves of strength you are intrinsically born with. Nothing wrong with taking care to look good…as long as that's not the be all and end all of your life. It is a means to an end. And, in the end, it matters only what kind of person you are; not how you look. Siya finally made sense of her own insecurities.

"Sorry, I'm late. My appointment at the salon took longer than I expected. I went in for one job and got several done!" Aisha's voice broke into her reverie. Looking up at her, Siya smiled. Taking in her white Lucknowi salwar kameez and ethnic silver jewellery, Siya marvelled at how stunning she looked. *It's so difficult to make out the struggles she has gone through. Wish I could erase some of them for her.*

"No problem. I was engrossed in my thoughts. You are glowing, Aisha!" As she stood up, Aisha enveloped her in a long, warm hug. Puzzled, Siya pulled away and asked, "Are you okay?"

"Yes! I'm absolutely fine, just nervous…really jittery."

"Oh…okay. Sit, sit. You want something to drink or eat?"

"Yeah. I need something to calm me…maybe I'll order one of their calming teas!" she said, beaming at Siya. Siya smiled back.

"So, why are you a bundle of nerves?"

Aisha's eyes lit up with adoration. "I can't believe I'll be proposing to Manav!" The light in her eyes faded as the lines on her forehead converged. Fingering the menu with her eyes lowered, she continued, "I've waited so long for this; I've moved mountains literally to get here so I can be with him forever. The years I've spent away from him have been the most despondent phase of my life. Going through the motions of marriage, domesticity, childbirth… all such a farce." Siya listened, finding herself unable to empathise.

"How can you call your life a farce? That's not…true," Siya added, trying to not get worked up, keeping her emotions at bay.

"Siya, my life so far has been dictated by others. My family wanted me to marry Neel, so I did. Neel wanted us to move to the US, so we did. He wanted us to have children, so I did. My heart was not in it…"

"Then why didn't you say so?"

"I couldn't, Siya. I was made to believe I was lucky he wanted to marry me! That is my biggest regret…," said Aisha in an anguished tone. "I'm a stronger person now. I know what I want. I don't want to live a life where I don't feel alive every moment. I want a life of passion and adventure. That is what I will have with Manav!"

"How can you be so sure?"

"Because I know the kind of person he is! It's so exciting being around him! He is not a boring intellectual...he's so much fun!" she sighed like a schoolgirl.

"Does Neel know?" Siya asked.

"Yes. He has known for a while...that my heart is not in this marriage. He doesn't know about Manav though. I don't know if I should tell him yet..."

"What's the hurry? You can always tell him after you come back," Siya suggested, buying time on Neel's behalf. *God knows how Neel is going to take this. Was this a good time to ask her about the kids? Strangely, she doesn't seem concerned about them. She is so wrapped up in herself and Manav.*

"Siya, Siya...Siyyyaaa!" Aisha's voice brought her back to the present. "I'm talking to you! What are you thinking?" she asked, petulantly.

"Sorry, Aisha. I've been a little stressed about the flash mob. I hope I don't muck up," said Siya, not letting her in on her thoughts.

"Oh, don't worry. You'll be good! I have confidence in you," she smiled, giving her hand a squeeze.

"Did I tell you that the Divas are part of the flash mob too?" Siya asked, mischievously.

"What? No way! They won't let you have anything for yourself!"

"Actually, I am the one who took them along."

"What? Why?" Aisha asked, mouth agape.

"They asked me to...very nicely, at that," she said gleefully, as she recounted the sequence of events leading up to their inclusion.

An hour later, when all that could have been shared was shared between them, Siya got up to go. A lot had been left unsaid. *Sometimes, it's better that way, no?* "All the best, darling," Aisha said, as she gave her a tight hug. "May you shine!" she added.

Siya didn't know if she should wish her luck too. Instead, she said, "Hope you find the happiness that's been eluding you."

As they walked out of the café together, Siya's heart fluttered strangely. She hoped that sense would prevail and Aisha would not do something foolish. *It's her life... to live.*

Delhi, 1996

What's love got to do with it—Tina Turner

The first time my husband proposed to me, I was not interested in marriage. He was handsome and well-placed with a bright future ahead of him. But, these things didn't matter to me then. I don't know what I wanted... I was battling demons of my own.

I had a colleague with the same name as my ex at work. I found it difficult to address him by his name. Sometimes, I wondered if he had picked up on it. Could people guess what I had been through by the way I walked or talked?

Once when we were sitting around at the lunch table, there was some gossip about a girl in the office having undergone an abortion. A heated discussion followed about whether she had done the right thing—morally, ethically etc. They had no idea what her reasons were and still, they judged her. No one talked about the boy and his responsibility.

I sat mutely and listened as the discussion went back and forth, torn between being a sinner (towards another life) and a saviour (of my own life). To quieten my inner turmoil, I ran to seek refuge in a quiet cubicle of the washroom. But I could not shut out the voice that kept repeating, "You are a killer. You took another life. You are a sinner, sinner, sinner..."

My husband persisted with his proposal, oblivious to the turmoil raging within me. My confidence those days was at an all-time low. I was surprised at his persistence. I debated with myself many times if I should tell him the truth. What if that turns him away from me? He was a very eligible man and would have plenty of girls lining up for him. And, me? I have a poor track record and am a bad judge of people. It would be stupid if I let him go. But, what if he realises the first time we...it's not as earth shatteringly painful as that. Who would know better than me? I can explain that easily... And that's how I married him.

35

As Friday the 13th dawned, the clock started ticking faster. The flash mob was scheduled for 6 pm on Sunday, the 15th of August (so there would be more people to watch) at Aromas.

Siya was so nervous with excitement that she even rehearsed at home, in front of the full-length mirror in her bedroom. Her boys sneaked in on her during one such session and doubled over with laughter! "Mama, you are dancing to 'Gangnam Style'? I didn't know you know this song!" snickered Aryan.

Hmmm, I can't let him know that I only heard it because of this dance. "Of course, I listen to new songs all the time! In the gym, on the radio, in the mall and pubs...your Mama is not so old," she said, sticking her tongue out at him. "Do old people dance in a flash mob, Aryan?" she asked.

"No way," he answered, matter-of-factly.

"Well, your mom is going to...does that make me young and cool?" she teased him.

"What? You are going to be in a flash mob?" he asked. "Will there be a lot of people watching? I hope none of my friends see it," he said, anxiously.

Siya picked up a pillow and threw it at him playfully. "How mean! Your mother is doing something that requires courage and you are not at all encouraging. Bad boy!"

"Mama, can I come to watch you? I promise I will clap for you," said Arjun, trying to make his mother feel better.

"Of course, you can. In fact, Papa will bring both of you to watch. I want all my boys to be there," she said, hugging them.

On Saturday morning, soon after rehearsal, the group broke out into excited chatter. "What should we wear? Should we all be in the same colours?" someone asked.

"No, no—it's a flash mob. We are supposed to just emerge from the crowd," offered another.

"I think this flash mob is the worst kept secret of Powai. Everyone knows it's happening! Everyone will be there to watch. It's not at all a surprise!" said another wise one.

"Ok, guys, calm down," said Manoj, clapping his hands to drown out any conversation. "Everyone will report here at 5 pm tomorrow. We will do one last rehearsal before we walk to the venue together. There will be some cameras to record this event, so please give it your best," he said, exiting the hall.

"I think we should wear bright colours, as in the video of this song," said Ira, addressing the group at large.

"Yes, that's a good idea," agreed someone.

"And, cool accessories like *dhinchak* sunglasses or footwear, something blingy!" chimed in Naina.

"Super! Let's do that. Express yourself...have fun," declared Prabha. "See you all tomorrow evening, folks," she said, wiping the sweat off her brow.

Walking back home with Naina and Ira, Siya was quiet as they discussed what they would wear in terms of clothes, accessories, and makeup. "I'm planning to wear that golden tube top I have...with the gold hoops and high heels. What about you, Ira?"

"I will wear the fuchsia pink top with my silver mini skirt. It'll look nice, no?" she asked.

"Oh yeah, you look pretty in pink. What about you, Siya? What will you wear?" she said, turning her gaze towards her.

"Oh, I don't know yet; will have to go home and ransack my cupboard to see what I have. I don't own any blingy clothes or accessories from what I remember," she said, speculatively.

"Oh, you can always borrow from me," said Ira instantly, making her almost jump.

"Thanks. I will. Let me first decide on my outfit," said Siya, unable to digest the generous offer. *Wow! That was unexpected,* she thought, smiling to herself.

The next morning, as Siya waited near the main gate for the divas to walk to the rehearsal venue; she was surprised to see Naina emerge from the porch all alone. "Hi! Ira won't be able to make it. She's not feeling well," she said, as she approached Siya.

"Oh, what happened? Everything okay, I hope?" she asked.

"No, not really...things have not been good between her husband and her. They have been having a lot of fights over some issues for a while."

"Oh, I'm sorry to hear that. She seems like a person who has it all under control," Siya remarked, as they started walking.

"Well, one cannot control everything all the time, right? Sometimes, things fall apart," she said.

Siya wondered again how difficult the lives of 'perfect' people can be. "Are they seeing a counsellor or somebody for help?" Siya asked.

"Does that help?" Naina asked, eyebrows raised sceptically.

"Well, it helps to understand some things better and put issues in perspective. It also depends on how dearly you want to resolve the problems," she said, her voice trailing off as she realised how it would have sounded.

"Ira can be quite hot-headed at times but she loves her son too much to put him through this trauma. Her husband is a nice guy. They are just two very different people who want very different things from life."

"In that case, counselling should help. In fact, a very close friend of Samar's is an excellent psychologist; I would be happy to connect them if she likes. Why don't you ask her? She may not like it, coming from me."

"That makes sense. I'll talk to her after rehearsal today," she said.

There was more commotion than normal that day. Lots of young people, mostly students, were milling around the place. Prabha's booming voice, however, could be heard over the commotion of the crowd. "People, we are going to rehearse in the open today. We need to organise our formation so we know who will stand at what spot tomorrow. Can you all gather around here please?"

Dropping their bags on the floor of the hall, everyone rushed out quickly. Prabha had figured out how well each person could dance. Going one by one, she assigned front rows to the fabulous dancers while others were placed in the back rows, depending on their agility and ability to remember the steps. As a result, Siya found herself somewhere towards the end while Naina was in the first row.

As the opening bars of the music started playing on the stereo system, a hush fell over the excited crowd. Faces appeared at the windows of the neighbouring houses. People were curious to see what was happening. As everyone swayed to the beats of the music, Prabha's voice could be heard leading them through the steps. Dancing out in the open was easier because everyone had more space to manoeuvre. No one was stepping on anybody else's toes as they did some times during practice inside the hall! It was nice to have an audience watching for a change. It made their effort feel more 'real'.

As the music ended, everyone assumed the final pose with a flourish, ecstatic at having pulled it off without a hitch. The neighbours burst into an appreciative applause, cheering the dancers. Naina surprised Siya by giving her a hug. *Whoa!*

"Well done, friends! Please remember there will be people watching us tomorrow—friends, family, cameras—let's rock it!" announced Manoj, standing atop a chair. Another round of woohoos and yays ensued at that. "Rehearsal at 4 pm after which we will all walk to the venue. Do tell your friends to come and watch. Share with as many people as you can. Remember, this is for Powai!" The crowd cheered and whistled enthusiastically.

Walking back home with Naina, Siya couldn't help sharing, "I can't believe this is really happening! It feels like a journey is coming to an end…makes me sad. This activity had kept me so charged and enthusiastic. After tomorrow, there will be nothing to look forward to."

"Don't worry, there will always be something else. You know, Siya, I have seen you change in the last couple of months. I'm sure you will find another challenge to focus on," Naina said, reassuringly.

"Hey, that's really nice of you. I hope Ira will be able to make it."

"Oh, she will not want to miss this opportunity. She'll be there," Naina said, with confidence.

Over dinner, Siya couldn't contain her excitement. In between mouthfuls of salad and grilled chicken, she shared with Samar how she was beginning to see the vulnerable and friendly side of the Divas. Keeping an eye on the boys to ensure they were not listening in, she said, "She even told me about the problems Ira is having in her marriage. I suggested connecting with a good counsellor"

"Really? Who?" he asked.

"Samar! Your dear friend, Imran. Who else do I know?" she said, rolling her eyes.

"Oh…but why are you getting involved, Siya? You don't even like her…," said Samar.

"I didn't like her because of the hurtful things she said to me. For some reason, she used to dislike me which is why I never warmed up to her. Listening to Naina talk about her problems, especially with regard to her child, made me feel sorry for her. She does not have it all figured out even though she appears to. I was only trying to help as a fellow human being. Nothing wrong with that, is it?" she asked.

Samar's eyes twinkled as he smiled at her. "Nope. Nothing wrong with that."

36

Independence Day is generally rainy and overcast in Mumbai as monsoon sets in full form by then.

Siya was awakened by the blaring of patriotic songs from a loudspeaker the next morning. As she realised that the tone was being set for Independence Day, she picked up her phone to check the time. There was a message from Aisha. As she clicked on the icon to read it, a smile played on her lips.

Big day for you! All the best, darling. Have fun. You will rock it!

PS: Big day for me too. I'm meeting Manav today!

Siya's smile faded. Her heart sank at the thought of Aisha meeting Manav. She couldn't fathom why. *It's Aisha's life, she can do as she wishes. Besides, they are both adults.*

Siya was soon distracted as she started getting everyone up and ready for the flag hoisting ceremony in the building lawns. Although dark clouds ominously hovered above, the ceremony was conducted solemnly followed by a modest breakfast, allowing residents to mingle with each other. Siya heard some of them talk about the flash mob but before she could volunteer more information, a light drizzle started, forcing everyone to scamper into the covered parking for shelter. Gradually, the gathering dispersed as everyone headed home.

At 4 pm, Siya was standing in front of the mirror in her bedroom. Dressed in a bright yellow halter neck top and jeans, Siya could not help but admire the result of her hard work...prodded by Aisha. Samar walked into the room just then. "Wow! You're looking sexy in that top! When did you buy it?"

"It was a gift from your sister. It didn't fit me then so I never wore it," she smiled as she turned around to face him.

"You're going to give the young ones a run for their money!" he exclaimed.

"Haha! It's not a competition; it's a collaboration. Hopefully, I'll fit in," she said, hugging him tightly.

"What's the matter? Are you nervous, Siya?" he asked, sensing more than just affection in the tightness of her hug.

Pulling away, she looked him in the eye. "I am nervous... but not for me."

"Then? For whom?" he asked.

"For Aisha."

"Aisha? Why?" he asked, concerned.

Sitting down on the easy chair, she motioned for him to sit on the stool facing her. Then, she told him how Aisha had not been able to get her ex out of her mind, how she had reconnected with him, how love had been rekindled, how she was going to meet him in Delhi to suggest they get together forever, how she was planning to leave her husband and kids to be with him.

When she stopped talking, she could see myriad questions on Samar's face. "Samar, I tried to talk sense into her but she is so besotted with this Manav and so obsessed with the idea of finally living her life on her own terms that she didn't like it one bit. I'm worried about what's going to happen...if he agrees or disagrees." As her eye fell on the clock, she jumped up like a spring. "It's 4:25 pm! I was supposed to report at 4:30...I better go. I'll see you out there with the boys," she said, pecking him on the cheek as she rushed out the door, picking up her handbag from the bed. Samar didn't move. He sat still, deep in thought.

37

As Siya rushed out of the elevator on the ground floor, she was surprised to see both Ira and Naina waiting for her at the main gate. Naina was dressed in a stylish denim jumpsuit that flattered her figure, accentuating her curvaceous waist and hips. Wedge heels added a retro charm to her outfit. Ira was dressed in a silver mini skirt and a fuchsia pink top. Long black boots reaching up to her knees added a lot of oomph. "Wow! You girls look so stylish! You could easily be shooting for a music video!" she exclaimed, surprised at how naturally the compliment came to her.

"You look fab in that top too!" Naina replied, grinning from ear to ear.

"Yup. Yellow suits you," Ira added, smiling self-consciously.

"What happened? What took you so long?" Naina asked, as soon as they started walking.

"I'm sorry. I just lost track of time while chatting with Samar," she replied.

Naina began rummaging through her handbag and fished out a pair of sparkly, golden sunglasses. "To add bling to your outfit," she said, holding it out.

"Wow! These are…shiny," she said, putting them on gingerly.

"Let me see," said Ira, turning Siya's face towards her. "Bling becomes you," she declared, with an approving smile.

"Thank you. I'll wear this once we are there," she said, sliding it inside the front pocket. *I can actually fit stuff inside the pocket of my jeans now—yippee!*

They entered the compound of Manoj's residence. It was buzzing with people. The air was electric, waves of enthusiasm rising in the air. People were standing around in groups, chatting excitedly. As Naina, Ira and Siya made their way inside, heads turned their way. *Why was everyone staring? Oh, how silly...I'm flanked by the Divas—I can bask in their glory!* Siya noted the appreciative glances that the Divas attracted. When Siya looked around at the crowd, she noticed that everyone was dressed in bright, glittering clothes and accessories. *I won't stick out if I put on those glasses here!*

As they entered the rehearsal hall, Prabha's booming voice was calling everyone to attention. "Take your positions, folks! Hurry, hurry. Let's do one quick rehearsal so we can head out fast." In a jiffy, the crowd scrambled around and reassembled in their assigned spots. The music started just as Prabha counted down to ten. A couple of bystanders cheered them on; the dancers couldn't help grinning as they gyrated. As the music ended, everyone assumed their finishing poses with a flourish, panting as they beamed.

Manoj appeared out of nowhere, clapping loudly. "Well done, guys! That was super. Now, let's see you up this outside on the streets!" Cheers and whistles resounded in the hall at his announcement.

As everyone started walking out of the main gate, towards Aromas, Naina and Ira gravitated towards Siya. "This is so exciting!" exclaimed Naina.

"I haven't felt such an adrenalin rush in a long time. Thanks, Siya," added Ira.

Siya was stunned. It was the last thing she'd expected. "You're welcome," she answered, with a smile.

Before they knew it, they were outside Aromas Café where a small crowd had gathered, in anticipation. A music system with amplifiers was placed along one wall of the café. A camera crew was stationed strategically opposite it. "Oh gosh, this is so surreal!" remarked Siya, in a dazed tone, taking in the camera crews that waited by the kerb.

"Let's rock it, girls," urged Naina in excited tones as they took their positions. Fortunately, the sun had shooed away the dark clouds from the morning and a gentle breeze was blowing. In a matter of minutes, the crowd swelled till there were some people actually standing on the railing of the café. Siya's eyes were scanning the crowd for familiar faces when a voice yelled out, "Mama!" Many female heads turned in the direction of the voice! Siya smiled as she realised it was Arjun calling out to her. She blew them a flying kiss. Samar signalled with a thumbs up as the music began.

Moving to the rhythm of the music, Siya had a spring in her step. She was happy she'd included the Divas in the flash mob despite her misgivings. It had felt like the right thing to do. With a beaming smile, she moved in tandem with her co-dancers, enjoying every step with gay abandon as the crowd cheered them on wildly. As the song ended, the dancers struck their final poses, perspiration shining on their foreheads. Siya's eyes searched the crowd as she tried to spot her family. Her eyes met Neel's who waved at her. She smiled back. The applause increased as the crowd chanted, "Once more, once more!"

Before they knew it, the music started again from the top as all the dancers looked at each other in disbelief. Murmurs of "What? Again? One more time?" could be heard all around. Not lacking in enthusiasm, they moved to the music as if in a trance, the steps coming naturally to all of them. Siya scanned the crowd, looking for her family. The cameras furiously clicked away even as some of those recording it moved with the crowd to capture them from different angles. It was so thrilling! Beaming at each other, everyone scrambled to high-five Manoj as the song ended.

Siya ran up to Samar, breathless but beaming. "How was it?" she asked, looking at the three men in her life.

"It was great! You guys have practiced a lot," Samar remarked.

"Mama, why were you not in the front row?" asked Arjun.

"Oh, because the best dancers are in the first row. I'm not such a good dancer," she admitted.

He didn't look convinced. "You were nice, Mama," said Aryan.

"Thank you, sweety," said Siya, giving him a tight hug.

"You were fabulous, Siya!" Siya turned around at the compliment and was pleasantly surprised to see Maya and Imran.

"Thank you so much, guys. I'm so happy you came," she said, as she was enveloped in a hug by both.

"We wouldn't have missed it. My friend here would have disowned me if I didn't show up to cheer his wife," said Imran, making a dig at Samar. Everyone laughed as Samar beamed, his dimples evidence of his delight.

"This calls for a celebration! Where shall we go for dinner?" asked Samar as the boys broke into a cheer at the idea. After debating between fast food joints, restaurants and cuisines, they finally agreed to go to the Italian restaurant, Prego, at the Renaissance Hotel, close to Powai.

"See you in the lobby in an hour" announced Samar, as they walked away in separate directions. Siya thought she saw Neel walking ahead. She wanted to call his name but wasn't sure it was him. "Isn't that Neel, Aisha's husband?" asked Samar.

"I think so," she answered, as she took in his measured gait and drooping shoulders. With his hands stuffed inside his front pockets, he walked with his head bent down... looking defeated. Just as Siya was about to call him, someone yelled her name.

Turning around, they saw Manoj walking furiously fast to catch up with them. Grinning from ear to ear, he pumped Siya's hand with gusto, saying, "Congratulations! We did it. Your idea was a runaway hit! Thank you!"

Siya blushed. Before she could say anything, Naina and Ira joined them, cheering for her. Siya went pink in the face. "Manoj, it was only an idea. You are the one who set it in motion, got so many people together and organised everything so beautifully. Right from the rehearsals to the choreographers to the music to arrangements at the venue, all the credit goes to you. So, many congratulations to you!" she said, giving him a hug, as Samar looked on.

It was Manoj's turn to blush. He mumbled an awkward 'Thank you' as they all bid him goodbye and walked away.

38

When Siya was getting dressed for dinner later, it struck her that she had not shared the news of the flash mob's success with Aisha. She called her but her phone was switched off. *When did Aisha say she would return—tonight or tomorrow? Maybe, she's on the flight now.* Immediately, she typed out a message.

Flash mob was a super duper hit! The crowd asked for an encore! Wish you were there to witness the excitement. We'll celebrate when you are back!

Siya smiled as she sent the message. *Aisha will be happy to know this.* Having got the boys to change, Samar walked into the bedroom to get dressed. Catching the smile on Siya's face, he asked, "Can't stop smiling, eh?"

"Nope," she answered, looking at him with a wide grin. "I just can't believe I was able to stand in front of all those people without losing my nerve. What's more, I actually remembered the steps in sequence and didn't fumble."

"You're forgetting your biggest achievement, Siya…" he said.

"What? Losing the kilos? I still have some to go actually… so my goal has not been achieved yet."

"No, I'm not referring to your weight loss."

"Then, what?"

"You have won over the Divas…"

Siya looked puzzled. "But, that was not my plan."

"Precisely. Including them in the flash mob was a master stroke!" he said, his tone appreciative.

"I didn't think about it like that, Samar. I was just trying to be inclusive. It would be so childish to let petty little grudges ruin the big picture."

"I didn't mean to say you were manipulative...you are evolving as a person. This weight loss journey has instilled confidence. You have become self-assured. You don't need a person or a job to endorse you; you are comfortable in your own skin," he said, pulling her closer, in a tight embrace.

Siya didn't know what to say. *This guy, I love him so much...* "It means a lot, coming from you. I wish Aisha had been here today. She is actually responsible for me even thinking about losing weight."

"Really? How's that?" he asked.

As she pulled out of the embrace, she said, "An offhand remark she made the first time I met her in Hiranandani. It just brought home the realisation with a bang—that I had let myself go. There's no logic to these things some times. The most innocuous comments can be life altering while the most pedantic statements can leave you unmoved."

Dinner with Maya and Imran at the Renaissance was what they had expected it to be—full of laughter, jokes, and many anecdotes. After the platters of pizza and bowls of pasta had been cleared, their kids wanted to explore the hotel. "Don't go to the swimming pool area, it's closed now. Stay close by so we can see you," Siya cautioned when Aryan asked if they could wander around.

As steaming cups of cappuccino replaced wine glasses, conversation veered to more adult topics. "Imran, you'll be receiving a call from a friend of mine—Ira," informed Siya.

"She's going through a rough patch. I thought talking to you would help," she explained.

Imran nodded as he took a sip of his coffee.

"Do let me know how it goes," she continued.

"I'm not at liberty to disclose information on my patients, Siya," he said, in a tone that conveyed professionalism.

"Oh, I'm sorry, I didn't mean to be intrusive," Siya said timidly, not wanting to invoke any stern remarks.

"I'm sorry, I didn't mean to sound harsh," he said.

"I understand. It's just that she's my neighbour, we live on the same floor. I hope she's able to resolve her issues and find peace."

"I'll keep that in mind," he said, smiling with his eyes.

The thought of Ira seeking help brought Aisha to her mind. *I wish Aisha had consulted Imran. Maybe, he could have made her see things differently. But Aisha does not want anyone telling her that she's wrong! She has just realised what she wants from life; her priorities have changed.* Siya felt that she could benefit from seeing a psychologist. A thirty-five year-old woman willing to leave her husband and kids for an ex flame needs to take some responsibility for the many lives involved. *A professional would have helped her… I, with my 'marriages are forever' mentality cannot wrap my head around it.*

"Siya… Siya," Maya's voice broke into her internal dialogue. "What are you thinking about so deeply?" she asked, touching her arm lightly.

Siya looked across the table at Samar who was engrossed in a conversation with Imran about investment options. She turned to face Maya. "You know my friend, Aisha, no?"

"Yes. What happened?"

"Nothing as yet...but I'm dreading what could. She has gone to meet her ex from college who she has been in touch with for a year or more. She believes she is still in love with him. She says she never loved her husband."

"Oh, that's huge!" Maya remarked.

Suddenly, all eyes turned on Siya. She looked at the faces waiting for her to continue. After a momentary hesitation, she realised that she was with people she could trust. "Yeah. Now, she wants to leave her husband and kids to be with him."

"What? You mean they want to get married?" Maya asked.

"She wants to marry him...and she's confident he wants the same. They had a chance to be together in college but it didn't work out and now, she wants to give him another chance."

"Hmmm...and, why does that worry you?" she asked.

"Because she has a decent, loving husband who may not be as handsome as her ex but he has given her everything she enjoys today."

"Do you mean creature comforts?" Maya challenged.

"Don't make it sound like that's not important, Maya. More importantly, he has given her love, respect, and security, which her ex never did. If he had loved her enough then, he would have made things happen. In my opinion, he's just a middle-aged man who is enjoying the attention he's getting from a very attractive woman. He has no long-term plans..."

"How do you know that?" asked Samar.

"She said she's going to ask him to marry her because he has not asked her yet! She is willing to leave everything for him! She's obsessed with him. God knows if he really loves her...or, is she only trying to fulfil unfulfilled desires which are past their expiry."

Samar was bristling to have a say. "Okay, I'm going to play the devil's advocate here. Maybe, when they were in college, he had nothing to offer her, so he backed off."

Siya chewed over it. "Could be...but, that was your past—good, bad or ugly—you have to make your peace with it. You cannot ruin your present by running after what you didn't get back then. You can't have it all."

"From what you've told me, she doesn't want to have it all. She only wants him," said Maya.

Siya suddenly remembered that Imran knew Neel from his time in America! Turning to him, she asked, "Imran, how well do you know Neel and Aisha?"

Imran paused to consider the question. "Not very well. We were neighbours when he was with Lehmann. We met at community events. When I bumped into him here, I invited him over for the first time. Although his wife seemed friendly back in the US, we didn't interact much on a personal level because we were all busy with our kids. She spent a lot of time in the gym. We saw her going from fat to fabulously fit in front of our eyes. Right, Maya?" he asked.

Maya nodded in affirmation. "Some dedication she had, despite having her hands full with two kids. Like a woman possessed!" she declared.

"That's how Siya has been lately! Absolutely consumed with losing the last two kilos," Samar interjected.

"Still struggling, Siya?" Imran asked with his eyebrows raised.

Siya's mind raced back to the conversation they had had on the subject in Aamby. "Well, I have an action plan which I'm going to put into motion. Let's hope it works," she smiled at him.

"Action plan? This sounds interesting...what do you have in mind?" Maya asked, rubbing her hands together in glee.

Siya laughed. "I'll tell you if you come shopping with me tomorrow!" she replied.

"Ooh, let's go," Maya said. "I'll pick you up at eleven," she offered.

The ladies picked up their handbags as the men rose to round up the kids.

39

As Samar was tucking into his breakfast the next morning, he asked Siya, "Why this sudden plan to go shopping with Maya?"

"Oh, I've been eyeing a dress at AND since I started my diet," she replied, absentmindedly, scanning the *Mumbai Mirror*.

"But, I thought you still have some kilos to go. What's the hurry?" he persisted.

Siya looked up from her paper. "I don't know how much longer that will take, Samar! What's the big deal? It's only a dress!" she retorted.

"I didn't say that is an issue. The urgency with which you want to buy it is," he yelled.

"What are you insinuating?" Siya hissed.

"You're smart enough to understand. I've warned you before, Siya—don't let your new avatar get to your head!"

"Oh, when you act differently with me thanks to the compliments from the opposite sex, it's okay. When I'm the one receiving it, I should keep my head on my shoulders," she huffed.

Samar pushed his plate away and walked out. Siya was baffled at his sudden explosion. *What's wrong with him today?*

Siya was pensive when she walked into the gym half an hour later. She was greeted with smiles and high fives by some members and trainers. *What's the matter with them?* she wondered. "*Arrey,* ma'am, you never told us. We would have joined in too!" announced Ajay, as she emerged from the lockers. Then, it dawned on her. *Oh, they have probably watched the video of the flash mob which went around yesterday.*

"I'm sorry, Ajay, it didn't strike me. I will remember next time," she promised.

"*Pucca, haan*?" he said, shaking her hand vigorously.

As she walked through the glass door to the cardio section, heads turned to look at her. "I saw you in the flash mob yesterday. You were good. You have lost so much weight! How did you do it?" asked a slightly plump young girl, sweating from her workout.

"Oh, a combination of diet and exercise," Siya answered, walking towards the treadmill before someone else could.

"I've been on Pooja Makhijani's diet for a month… I've only lost two kilos. How did you do it?" she asked, desperately.

"That's a very good beginning! Just stay strong and don't give up on yourself," Siya encouraged her, as she pressed Start.

After a quick shower at home, Siya got dressed. She was still trying to unravel what had upset Samar but she didn't let that dampen her enthusiasm for shopping! Her heart was set on the sexy black dress she had seen at AND. While Aisha and her group of slim friends had tried on various garments, she had just watched and sighed. *There's no way I'm going to fit into any of these clothes without looking like a buffalo oozing out, desperate to fit in with the 'it-crowd'*, she had thought then. *However, I am much slimmer now. Besides, I have a very good reason to buy it. I have to blow his mind when he sees me!*

As she pulled on a new pair of Tommy Hilfiger jeans that fit her beautifully, complimenting her toned legs and slim waist; she looked at her reflection—*Nothing like a pair of well-fitted jeans! Dress it up or dress it down and you know you're looking good.* Pulling on an off-white strappy spaghetti top with peacock motifs all over, she scrambled in her jewellery box for a pair of silver earrings with a woven silk thread pattern in the colours of a peacock. Standing back, she admired how beautifully the earrings matched the top. Pulling out an indigo blue eye pencil, she drew a line on her eyelids. A silver wrist cuff completed the look, as she dabbed on some tinted lip balm on her lips. She was taking extra care to dress up this morning because she was going out with Maya, who was always so well put together. She rummaged in her cupboard for a silk handbag that she had not used in a while. It had ethnic block print motifs all over in blue, red, and ivory. *Maya will love this,* she thought as she switched items from one handbag to another. *Wallet, sunglasses, keys, lip balm, cell phone.* Walking out of the house, she gave last minute instructions to Vaishali on picking up the kids from school in case she was delayed.

As Siya walked out of the lift on the ground floor, Maya's car pulled into the porch. She looked gorgeous in a kalamkari salwar kameez which she had teamed up with oxidised silver jewellery. "You look gorgeous, Maya! I love your jewellery—it's exquisite!" said Siya.

"Look at you, Siya! You look like a PYT—who will believe that you are a mother of two kids! I feel so old suddenly," she said, pouting dramatically, for effect.

"Rubbish! You don't look a day older than twenty-five!" Siya tried to pacify her.

"You are such a sweetheart to say that. So, tell me, what's your plan? I'm really intrigued after your announcement last night."

"Remember I told you about meeting my ex?" Maya nodded. "Well, he's coming to Mumbai this week."

"Oh, okay," she said.

Maya waited for Siya to continue but she didn't say another word, she just looked out of the window as if to avoid eye contact. Maya placed her hand over Siya's. Siya turned to look at Maya, unsure of what to say. "Maya, I'm not looking for romance or a fling of any sort. I'm looking for answers, I need closure."

"He hurt you deeply, didn't he?" she asked, kindly.

"Yes, he did. And, I didn't realise how deep it was because I had blocked it from my mind...but it continued to reside in my subconscious somewhere. Only when Imran asked me to introspect and address the blocks in my own body, did I realise this. I had to go through the most terrifying episode of my life alone because of him. Despite knowing that, he never showed up. He made a perfunctory call to enquire but he never arrived at my doorstep, announcing eternal love and declaring that he couldn't live without me! He, who had once wanted to grow old with me, didn't pursue me even once after I said I didn't want to meet him. He took the easy way out; he slinked away. Liar..." muttering the last word under her breath.

"Are you going to confront him?" Maya asked.

"I don't know...I'm not sure. What I do know is that he lives alone. He's not married. He is living today with the choices he made yesterday. I want him to regret his choices. I want him to regret letting me go. I want him to see me as I am today and realise that he could have had a life with me if only... I want him to realise that it's not nice to break someone's heart and shatter their confidence." Siya exhaled deeply, as if to expel the bitterness.

"You surprise me, Siya. I would have never guessed your line of thinking. Somehow, I don't associate vengefulness with you," Maya declared, solemnly.

"It's not, Maya. If I was seeking revenge, I would have flirted shamelessly with him, led him to believe that I am still hankering for him and then refused to meet him when he came into town! But, that's not my agenda," she said, smiling shyly at Maya.

"Well, good on you, Siya! You're a gutsy girl. Does Samar know?" she asked, as the car stopped at the entrance of the shopping mall.

Siya nodded. "He knows that he was my boyfriend in college. No more. I didn't think it would help to share more when we got married. And I'd anyway buried it deep down so I didn't have to think about it…"

"Don't mind what I'm going to say, Siya, because it's coming from a place of concern. I know this is going to sound like a cliche but honesty is key to a successful marriage. If it matters so much to you then Samar will understand. From what I've seen, he's a mature man who'll deal with it sensibly."

"All in good time, Maya. Let me do this for me now." Maya smiled as she squeezed Siya's hand. Just knowing that she had Maya's support gave her a surge of confidence!

As they walked into the mall together, Maya linked her arm in Siya's as she said, "Let's go find a killer outfit that will shroud the rest of his days in a pall of gloom."

40

Siya turned left as they walked into the mall. She knew exactly where she wanted to go, for a change. At any other time, she would have sauntered along, window shopping, even though she knew what she truly wanted. She was a proverbial Cancerian in the sense that she got to her goal sideways, never head on.

As they walked into the AND store, the salesgirl politely greeted them. While Siya made her way to the rack that held all their apparels in black, Maya browsed around. Siya patiently went through the clothes, one by one, till she came upon what she was looking for—the halter neck black dress with little pearl embellishments on the loop around the neck! She pulled it out excitedly, happy to have found it. The fabric of the dress was as soft as a whisper. "Maya, what do you think?" Siya asked, holding the dress out for her to see.

"That's a sexy dress, Siya! I think it'll look fabulous on you—go ahead and try it!" urged Maya.

Siya asked the shop assistant to bring her the dress in a size that would fit. The girl scurried to the back of the store as Siya joined Maya in admiring the accessories on display. "This is so beautiful!" exclaimed Maya, holding out a pair of silver hoops encrusted with little crystals. "It'll go very well with your black dress," she added.

Siya smiled. "It is beautiful! Let me try it with the dress and see," she said.

"Ma'am, here it is," said the shop assistant, holding out a Size 6 dress.

Siya rushed to the trial room, she couldn't wait to try it on. Turning to face the only wall in the small cubicle, she took off her top and jeans. Muttering a silent prayer, she unzipped the dress from the left and slipped it on. With her eyes shut, she felt the dress cascade over her head and shoulders as it came to rest just below her knees. *This feels so utterly, butterly delicious!* As her hands went around the back of her neck to button the halter loop, she turned around to face the mirror. Patting the dress in place, she opened her eyes, reluctantly. She did a little pirouette, keeping her eyes on her reflection, as the dress swayed gracefully, making her feel like she was waltzing in a ballroom! She quickly put on the earrings. They matched beautifully! *I have to show this to Maya!*

Siya opened the door and stepped out. Maya was engaged in conversation with the shop assistant. Both heads turned to look at Siya simultaneously. "Wow!" Maya exclaimed even as she let out a throaty whistle. Siya laughed a heady laugh.

"Ma'am, this dress is looking very nice on you," the assistant remarked.

"Nice? She is going to blow his socks off! This was made for you, Siya. Just buy it!" she encouraged. Siya grinned foolishly as she told the assistant she would take it.

Walking back into the trial room, she gave herself a good look in the mirror. *You've come a long way, Siya!* Feeling truly proud of what she had achieved, Siya unzipped the dress and slipped out of it. Just then, her cell phone buzzed. She scrambled to put on her clothes as she fished the cell phone out of her handbag. Holding it in the hollow of her neck as she pulled up her jeans, she answered, "Hi! Who is this?"

"Hi, Siya. This is Sara, a friend of Aisha's. Remember we all went out shopping together?"

"Oh, yes! I remember! How are you?"

"I'm okay. I'm calling about Aisha…"

"Oh, is she back? What happened? Don't tell me she had another fall—she is quite the Calamity Jane!"

"Siya, I don't know how to tell you this but Aisha is no more."

"WHAT? Is this a joke or something? I just met her before she left for Delhi. She was absolutely fine. She was so excited about her trip."

"Siya, Aisha killed herself by overdosing on sleeping pills. She was depressed, I believe."

"That can't be true…it's not possible. Aisha is a fighter…"

"I know. We can't believe it either. Neel thought you should know since you were one of her closest friends." The phone dropped out of her hand as Siya slumped on the floor.

A million thoughts buzzed around in Siya's head. *Why would Aisha do that? What happened in Delhi? What did Manav say to her? Did Neel find out? It's my fault. I should have stopped her from going to Delhi. But, how can you be so sure that that was the reason for her…*

"Siya! Are you still admiring yourself in the dress?" called Maya's voice with a hint of a smile, even as she continued to knock on the door.

Siya was jolted out of the world she had travelled into. Looking around, she realised she was sitting sprawled out on the floor with her handbag, dress, and cell phone in her lap. She placed the dress on the stool next to her as she pulled herself up. She unlatched the door and walked out, looking distraught. "Siya, what happened? Is everything okay?" asked Maya, noticing the downcast expression. Siya ran into her arms as tears rolled down her face. Maya instinctively hugged her right back. "What's the matter, darling? Tell me please." Maya persisted.

"Aisha is no more," she mumbled, with her face pressed into the cradle of her shoulder.

"What?" asked Maya, incredulously, pulling her away so they were facing each other.

"I just got a call from a friend of hers, saying that she committed suicide. It's my fault, Maya, I should have stopped her from going to Delhi and meeting Manav. I was so concerned about losing her friendship…now, I have lost her forever." Siya said, bursting into tears again as she slumped against a wall, her hands covering her face.

Calling out to the shop assistant, Maya requested for a glass of water. Handing it to Siya, she said, "Calm down. It's not your fault. God alone knows what prompted her to take such a drastic step… Would you like to go over?" Siya nodded, mutely. Beckoning the shop assistant to pack up the black dress, Maya handed her credit card over. Holding Siya by the arm, she collected her card and shopping bag as she guided her out of the store. Calling the driver on the phone as they walked towards the exit, she instructed him to bring the car around. Walking past the beautiful displays in the shop windows, Siya thought how strange life was. *I walked in happy and confident and I'm walking out feeling rotten and guilty—we can never tell what's going to happen in the next moment.* As they sat in the car, Maya handed Siya a box of tissues.

Wiping away her tears, Siya took a deep breath. "Thank you, Maya," she said, giving her hand a gentle squeeze.

41

As they drove into Hiranandani, Siya guided the driver to Aisha's building. She had butterflies in her stomach, not sure how it would be at her apartment. I can't do this alone. I must call Samar and ask him to come. *Even after how he left this morning, Siya? Yes! I need him now.* Bringing her phone out of her bag, she dialled his number. Samar, however, had not forgotten. "Yes, Siya, I'm in a meeting. Is this urgent?" he asked, in a grim tone.

"Samar, Aisha is no more," she said, trying to control herself from breaking down.

"What? What do you mean? What happened?" he asked, concerned.

"I don't know. I'm going to her place. Can you please come?"

"Sure. I'll try to be there as soon as possible. Are you going there alone?" he asked, concern for her well-being upper most in his mind.

"No. Maya is with me. Shall I wait for you in the lobby?"

"Yes, do that. Give the phone to Maya," he said.

Siya handed over the phone to Maya. "Of course, Samar. Don't worry, I'll stay with her till you come. No problem at all. I will, I will," she said, as she disconnected the call and handed the phone back.

As Siya waited on a bench in the lobby with Maya in tow, many people passed by. She nodded perfunctorily as she recognised some faces from the complex. A stream of people wearing sombre expressions walked into the building. Siya guessed them to be Neel's colleagues. Maya nudged Siya gently as she said, "Are you okay, Siya?"

"How can I be okay? I should have had the guts to say what I felt when it was required. I was so spineless," she sighed, cupping her mouth with one palm. Maya patted her arm gently.

"Siya, isn't it?" said a female voice, making Siya look up.

"Yes, Sonia, right?" she said, recognising her as Aisha's friend from the shopping spree.

"So sad about Aisha, *na*? I've just been upstairs; Neel is completely shattered. It must have been horrifying for him to see her like that, no? Her body is so bloated from the overdose." Siya cringed. "I wonder why she did it. Even though they were very different people, he worshipped the ground she walked on; at least that's what he made it seem like," and she went on and on, offering opinions without being asked, passing judgement callously. Siya could not believe that Sonia was a friend of Aisha's. *How could she be so insensitive? How could she discuss this like the plot of a novel? Did she have no respect for the departed... Departed? Oh my God, is that what Aisha is now?*

Just then she heard her name being called out loud. Turning around, she saw Samar rushing towards her. She ran to hug him and held on, tightly, forgetting all about their tiff. Samar held her for a while and then whispered, "Shall we go up?" Siya looked at him with shock. And then, she nodded timidly, realising that she could not avoid it. Samar went over to thank Maya. "Would you like to come up?" he asked.

"Not now. I'll come later with Imran. Let me know when the prayer meeting is scheduled for." Maya answered.

She hugged Siya before leaving, "Take care of yourself. Let me know if you need anything," Siya nodded sadly, as she walked towards the elevator with Samar.

Travelling upward, Siya's mind wandered to all the times she had visited Aisha. Their endless chatter over cups of green tea and coffee. The time they had had a minor tiff…the first time she had bumped into her at the exhibition gallery… As the lift stopped, Samar walked out with Siya following close behind. She clutched his hand to slow him down. As they walked towards Aisha's apartment, they saw a group of people thronging the doorway. Siya's heart started beating so loudly that she was afraid everyone could hear it. Muttering 'excuse me', Samar pulled her along inside the apartment. Siya started perspiring as a pall of white descended over her eyes. Her breathing became ragged as her gaze swept over the faces in the room, staring pointedly at the floor. As it came to rest in the centre of the room, she saw a once familiar face lying on the floor. Siya's heart sank as her legs buckled under her. She fell with a thud to the sound of gasps.

When she came to, a while later, she found herself propped in a chair in the balcony. Samar was standing next to her, fanning her face with a newspaper. Feeling confused, she reached out to stop it. Samar looked down at her. "Siya! Are you okay?"

"What happened, Samar? All I remember is feeling light headed as I sank into quicksand…"

"Siya, we are at Aisha's where she…"

"Oh! She's in there, right? I remember now. I can't go in, Samar; I don't want to see her like that," she said, as she burst into tears, clinging to him for support.

"It's okay, you don't have to go in there," said a male voice, sombrely. Siya looked up to see Neel standing at the entrance of the balcony. Dressed in a designer white shirt and blue jeans, his eyes were red and puffy, his expression distraught, his spirit seemed shattered. "I cannot understand why Aisha left…like this. She was perfectly fine last night. We had a couple of glasses of wine as we do on weekends. She was telling me about her Delhi trip. This morning when she didn't wake up, I thought she was tired and wanted to sleep in. It was only when the maid called me at work to say that she wasn't responding at all… I know I was not good enough for her but was it so terrible living with me that she had to leave like this?" he asked them, his pain clearly visible on his face.

Siya broke away from Samar and hugged him. *Nobody deserves to be made to feel like this.* She didn't console him or offer any words of solace. They were two people who had loved Aisha dearly. They were angry at what she had done. They felt betrayed and hurt.

"Neel, the police are here. They want to speak with you," said Samar, placing a hand on his shoulder, as someone from inside signalled to him. He pulled out of Siya's arms, lifting his specs as he wiped the tears away.

"What do they want?" he asked in irritation.

Siya turned to Samar for an answer as Neel walked away. "The society office must have informed them since it's a suicide. There's a process that needs to be followed," he explained. Siya's face fell further. "Why don't you go home? I'll see you there later," he said.

"I'm not going inside, I can't," her lips trembled and her throat choked with every word.

"Okay, okay. Take your time," he consoled, leaving her to check on what was happening inside.

Siya waited on the balcony. Her mind was blank as she stared into the hills beyond. "The police are taking her body for a post mortem," Samar said, joining her after a while.

"Post mortem? But, why?" Siya asked, wondering if they would mutilate her body.

"Since it was a suicide, they have to rule out foul play. Besides, no note has been left behind so anyone could be a suspect," Samar whispered.

Siya was shocked! "Oh my God! Who would do this to Aisha? Do they think Neel could have?" her voice trailed off.

"Don't vex yourself, Siya. Go home. The driver is downstairs. I'll also come in a bit," he urged her.

Even though some people hung around to commiserate with Neel, the maids were scurrying to clean up the floor where the body had been laid. The tears had dried on most faces although sadness still remained. The intervention by the police had led to whispered conversations in corners even as the house was shrouded in an eerie kind of silence. Siya quickly made her way to the main door, avoiding eye contact with Neel lest he saw her guilt. She was anxious to get away from the visions that were playing havoc with her mind.

42

Vaishali opened the door when she rang the doorbell. The kids were back home from school; she could hear them in their room. They ran out when they realised Mama had returned. "What did you get us, Mama?" Arjun asked, hugging her, because that's what she did every time she went shopping with her friends. She always brought back something for them—books, toys, doughnuts, cookies, chocolates—to assuage the guilt of a mother who has been indulging herself.

"Nothing, baby. Mama didn't have any time to look around," she answered, even as Vaishali admonished them.

"Mama has just come back; she's tired. Let her rest." Siya's face shot up. As her brows creased in puzzlement, Vaishali answered, "Bhaiya had called to tell me. He told me to fetch the kids from school."

Oh! Thank God Samar reminded Vaishali...the kids would have gotten really anxious otherwise. She smiled weakly at Vaishali. "Do you want to have lunch?" she asked.

"Oh, it must be past lunch time, *na*?" Siya asked, looking up at the Roman numbered clock in the dining room. It was 3:15. "I'm going to have a bath first, then I'll have a cup of tea. You've eaten *na*?" Siya asked as Vaishali nodded in affirmation.

After a quick shower, Siya had her tea with a sandwich, sitting with the kids as they watched cartoons on TV. She nibbled on it listlessly as different thoughts jumped around in her mind. "What happened, Mama? You're not going to scold us for not changing out of our uniforms?" asked Aryan, as he watched her listless expression.

"Hmmm...baby, a friend of mine left me today," she answered, absentmindedly.

"Was she your best friend, Mama?" Arjun chipped in with another question.

"Yes, she was. When we were in school, she was my best friend."

"Where has she gone, Mama? Is it too far for you to go?" asked Aryan.

"Yes, it's far away."

"She must have gone to the US. You can call her on Skype and talk to her every day, like you do with *Maasi*," answered Arjun innocently, believing it a solution that would make his mother happy.

Siya smiled. "I love you boys," she said, hugging them both close to her, tightly. *Did Aisha think about her kids? Did it not bother her that she would be leaving them for good? Maybe, she didn't love Neel enough but her kids... Why did you do it, Aisha? What made you take such a drastic step?* "Boys, Mama is going to lie down for a while. Can you please keep the volume down?" she said, kissing them on the top of their heads as she got up to leave. Her head was buzzing with a million questions that no one but Aisha could answer.

As she walked into her bedroom, she noticed an AND shopping bag lying on the floor. *How did this get here? Maya must have dropped it off. I would have been a mess if I had been all by myself when I got the call. Thank God for Maya...* In an effort to distract herself, she picked up the book lying on her bedside—Vikram Seth's *An Equal Music*. It was the story of an affair between a married woman and her ex. Both were talented musicians; hence, the writer had spent reams of pages elaborating on the nature of music compositions they played. Siya didn't understand the technicalities of music at all but it was the love angle that had kept her hooked. She wanted to know how it would end. Would Seth make her leave her husband and child for her ex-lover? Or, would she do what all heroines in films did—be the righteous wife by sacrificing passion and happiness at the altar of duty and family? As she resumed reading from the page she had last read, a particular sentence popped out—*People who have a before and after should know that you can't relive your life.* Siya was transfixed. *Was Aisha trying to relive her 'before' life?*

Her eyes strayed outside the window to the lake. The sun had come out after two days of continuous rain. Sunlight danced on its surface playfully, creating a shimmering pattern. Siya gasped. It was such a beautiful sight that it hurt her eyes to continue staring. She looked away, feeling momentarily blinded. Her eyes flitted over objects inside her room, in an effort to cool her eyes. They came to rest on the AND bag. *The sexy black dress! Have I not been trying to relive my before even though my after is all that I've ever wanted?* The ringing of the doorbell broke into her reverie. *Who could it be at this time? Must be one of the boy's friends,* she thought. As the clip clop of heels neared her bedroom, she turned around, surprised to see Samar walking in. He looked flushed and exhausted. "Did anything else happen?" asked Siya, reaching out to hug him.

Samar held his hand up saying, "No, not really." Siya nodded, as she waited for him to answer. "It was heart wrenching, Siya. Neel broke down when people were discussing how to retrieve the body for cremation…some people don't help one bit, in such situations. The questions they ask, the things they say; but most of all, it's what they don't say out loud that hurts the most. I feel really terrible for him. I'm really upset with your friend," he said.

Siya sighed. "That makes two of us," she said. "I'd like to go and meet Neel and the kids later. I didn't say a word to any of them. Will you come with me?" she asked, hoping he would say yes.

"Of course. Let me shower and change," he said, making his way to the bathroom.

43

As they entered Aisha's apartment later that evening, dusk had begun to creep into the house, enlarging their shadows as they walked in. Neel was sitting on the sofa in the drawing room, surrounded by people. The minute he laid eyes on them, he stood up as if to escape. "Thank you for coming. I will definitely reach out if I need any help. Please excuse me for now," he said. They nodded sympathetically and rose to leave. Siya acknowledged them as she spotted some friends of Aisha in the motley crowd. In no mood to make conversation with any of them, she kept her eyes lowered as they exited.

Once they were out of earshot, she looked around to make sure no one else was around. Apart from the domestic help, she spotted no one. "I'm so sorry, Neel. For our loss," she said, reaching out to clasp his hand.

He smiled sadly. "It feels like this is a nightmare and I'm going to wake up any minute to her voice or laughter." Tears welled up automatically in both of their eyes. Fighting hard to push them back, he asked, "Do you know why she did it?" Siya nodded her head in negation. "That's what is eating me up. Why did she do this? Who or what pushed her? I wish she had just left me for whoever she wanted... but not like this," he said, looking down at their hands clasped together.

"Why would you think there's somebody else?" Siya asked gingerly, not sure if he knew anything.

"Siya, I'm not a fool. I've known Aisha for long enough to know she didn't really love me. She played her roles well—wife, mother, daughter-in-law; but, her heart was elsewhere. I could not win over her heart," his voice cracked as he quietened. Siya looked at Samar pointedly but he shook his head.

"Where are the kids?" Samar asked, trying to veer the conversation away to a safer topic.

"They have gone over to play at a friend's house. Fortunately, they were away at school when this happened. They didn't even see her one last time. How could I let them see her like that? She looked nothing like the Aisha they knew..." he sighed.

"I can understand. But, you should have a chat with them—I'm sure they have a lot of questions. It's best you answer them before someone says something unpleasant," Samar answered. Neel nodded.

"It may be a good idea to have someone from the family around when you do," Siya said.

"Yeah, you're right. They are quite fond of Arunima, their aunt. Having her around will be a big help."

"Arunima is here? It's been so long since I last saw her. Where is she?" Siya asked, excited at the prospect of meeting Aisha's sister who had been witness to their childhood friendship.

"She's in the guest room. Let me get her for you," Neel said, getting up from the sofa.

"Arunima is Aisha's elder sister. She was the quieter of the two. She never hung out with us but she was always there in the background," said Siya, as she filled Samar in.

Arunima walked into the hallway beside Neel. She was the same height as Aisha and her features had a striking resemblance too. "Hello," she said, sombrely, shaking hands with Samar and Siya, as if they were meeting at an official conference. Siya instinctively hugged her.

"I'm sorry I couldn't help myself. Do you remember me? I used to hang out a lot with Aisha," trying to keep her tone from sounding enthusiastic or cheery lest she think Siya wasn't sad about the recent turn of events.

Arunima looked hard and muttered a soft, "Yes, I do. Aisha and you used to be like peas in a pod." There was an awkward pause. "Wish we were meeting in happier circumstances though."

"We are very sorry for your loss," offered Samar, trying to fill the silence.

Arunima smiled in acceptance of their condolence message. "It's nice to know Aisha had so many friends," she said, a Zen-like smile playing on her lips.

"Unfortunately, no one knew her well enough to know why she…" Neel's voice faltered, leaving the question hanging in the air.

"Don't hassle yourself so much over it, Neel," said Arunima as she reached out to touch his arm, stealing a glance at Siya.

"How can I not, Nima? A man deserves to know why his wife preferred death over him, no?" he lashed out. Everyone gasped as they stepped back automatically. With imploring eyes, he turned to Siya. "Did she never tell you anything? About our differences causing friction? My constant harangue with her to be connected and in sync with her family?"

Siya was stumped at his directness. She instinctively looked at Arunima for help. Before she could utter anything, Samar reached out to calm him. "I'm sure there is an explanation, Neel. You need to look for it. We are here to help you. Just tell us how." Neel nodded dispiritedly.

Tears streaming down her face, Siya hugged Neel. She could completely understand his helplessness at Aisha's rejection. "Please let us know if we can be of any help in the coming days," she offered.

Patting Neel on his back, Samar asked, "Any news from the police? When will they release the body?"

Neel let out a long sigh. "I'm going to have to pull some strings to make it happen soon. It would be disrespectful to leave her there. I'm sure the autopsy report will not reveal anything else."

As they walked towards the door, Arunima touched Siya's shoulder. "When did you last meet her?" she asked.

"Just before she left for Delhi. She was so excited about her trip..." and she stopped fearing she would reveal more than was required. "Maybe, it's best to remember her like that—happy and excited." Siya gave her a small smile as they entered the elevator.

"Do you think she knows?" Samar asked Siya as soon as the elevator started descending.

"I think so...but, I'm not sure. Can't even ask her outright" she humpfed.

Later that night, Maya called to check how Siya was doing. "I'm okay now...just really perturbed," Siya answered.

"Don't dwell too much on it. The truth will come out sooner or later," Maya advised.

"Maya, I'm sure it has something to do with her Delhi trip. The only one who can tell me is not here anymore. I feel guilty for not having stopped her from going."

"Siya, our minds are very powerful. They can make a hell out of heaven and a heaven out of hell, depending on the choices we make. Aisha made her choice based on what her heart desired. Just like you and me. It's not easy to choose what is right over what 'feels' right." She paused to let her words sink in. "By the way, I had your dress sent over to your place. Hope you got it?" she asked, in an effort to divert her attention.

"Yes, I did." Siya answered absent-mindedly, not willing to think about it. Her mind was buzzing with thoughts of Aisha. "Thank you for everything, Maya. I'll hang up now; I'm feeling exhausted."

"Sure, Siya. Take care. Goodnight. Call me whenever you feel like it," said Maya, hanging up.

Siya slept restlessly that night. She couldn't get Aisha's face out of her head. She had looked so beautiful and sounded so happy and nervous the last time they had met. Aisha had encouraged her to get out of her comfort zone, recognise her own strengths and follow her heart. Siya lay awake thinking about all the ways in which she had changed her life. *Encouraging me to connect with Siddhant was very perceptive too. She probably sensed there were questions in my subconscious I was seeking answers to, so I could achieve closure.*

In the eerie stillness of the night, Siya could sense Aisha's presence. *Maybe, she was still seeking…something had made her so unhappy that she couldn't bear to live anymore.* The smallest sound would make Siya sit up in bed. Siya's gaze travelled over all the objects in the bedroom. The curtains seemed to be hiding something in the pleats of darkness… she clenched her eyes shut, afraid that she would see Aisha if she opened them.

44

The next morning, Siya woke up to the sound of Samar whistling as he got dressed. "What time is it?" she asked, sitting up in bed. Raising her eyes to the clock, she shrieked, "It's eight-thirty! I have to wake up the kids and get them ready for school! Oh God, how come my alarm didn't go off?" she asked, pushing the Jaipuri quilt away in anger.

"Relax, Siya. The kids left for school a while back. Between Vaishali and me, we got everything done," said Samar, holding her by the shoulders, to calm her down. "You had a rough day yesterday...why don't you sleep in?" he offered.

"Sleep? That's eluding me. I couldn't sleep last night. I just kept thinking about her and seeing her face."

"I know. I heard you muttering in your sleep. Listen, just relax today. Go for a massage. Watch a movie, listen to music, bake something yummy. Cheat on your diet!" he suggested, smiling that twinkly smile, as he pulled her into his arms and kissed her forehead. "Bye. I'll see you in the evening. Call me if there's anything," he said, releasing her as he walked towards the door.

"What about your lunch?" Siya asked, suddenly remembering that she had given no instructions the night before.

"I'll order something at work," he replied, walking out of the door.

"Oh," she said, feeling guilty at her poor planning.

"Didi, I made him a good breakfast of parathas with eggs. Don't worry," Vaishali called out from behind, trying to appease her.

Turning around, she looked at her and smiled. "What would I do without you?" she asked, placing a hand on her arm.

"Let it be. Tell me now, what do you want for breakfast? The same as Bhaiya?"

Siya pondered for a bit. "Sure, why not? I'll cheat a little today! Make me some lukewarm water with honey and lemon first; I'll go to the gym and come," said Siya, making her way to the bathroom.

Siya went through the motions of her workout like a robot. "What happened, ma'am? Are you unwell?" asked Ajay, watching her walk listlessly on the treadmill.

"I'm okay, Ajay. Didn't sleep well last night. Maybe, that's why I'm low on energy today," she answered.

"Go home then. Listen to your body. Give it what it needs. Don't force it to do something else," he advised.

Pushing the Stop button on the treadmill, she smiled at him weakly. "You're right. I need some rest today. See you tomorrow," she said, waving at him.

"Ma'am, some members were talking about a gym member's suicide in Octavius yesterday. Have you heard of it?" he asked, probing for information.

Siya was stunned. "Yes, she was a very dear friend of mine." Siya answered, enunciating every word so he would get the message.

"Oh, I'm sorry...take care," he said, suitably embarrassed.

As she walked back home, she marvelled at the human psyche. *How we wait for misfortune to fall on a person so we can discuss it with gusto; secretly relieved it wasn't us. What's sad is that more often than not, it is our own friends who indulge in it.*

As she entered her home, the aroma of parathas being roasted on a hot griddle evoked hunger in her. She was so touched that Vaishali was eager to provide comfort in whatever way she could. "Oh God, that smells so good! I don't remember when I last had parathas for breakfast!" she said, devouring the plate of food that was set out.

After a soul satisfying breakfast, Siya moved to the easy chair in her room, nursing a cup of tea. *Let's see what's happening in the world outside,* she thought, bringing out her laptop and logging into Facebook. The message icon was flashing red but she couldn't tear her eyes away from the newsfeed. As she scrolled down, she was aghast to see condolence messages on Aisha's wall. "You will be missed, Aisha", "What a pity that such an effervescent life was snuffed out like this", "May God grant courage to Neel and the kids to cope with this tragedy" ...and so on and so forth. Some of the messages were from her friends who lived locally, others she didn't know. *Boy, news sure travels fast on social media. I wonder how Neel is dealing with this,* she thought, absently clicking on the message inbox. It was a message from Siddhant...

Hi! I'm coming into Mumbai in two weeks! I would love to see you as soon as I land...please let me know if it's possible. I will be there for the whole week (including the weekend), so we can meet often. Often may also not be enough though. Haha! I'm really excited, Siya. See you soon!

She smiled wryly. *If only he had shown half the excitement when it was required of him... He has already assumed that I will see him often...will I? Is that what I want? I have led him to believe that I want to see him; which is why he is making this trip.*

Don't flatter yourself, Siya—he says he's here on work. Rubbish! His curiosity is piqued, he's eager to see me; work is just an excuse. You have a sexy new dress too! He'll be eating out of your hands… Ok, ok—I need time to think this through. Pipe down…

In an effort to channelise her thoughts elsewhere, Siya logged out of Facebook. She logged into her email and scrolled down the inbox. She clicked open a mail from school and began to read it. *Janmasthami celebration…dress rehearsal, invitation…*the next mail she opened was a collection of healthy and low-calorie recipes from Tarla Dalal. *Aah! Kala chana salad, cucumber soup, multigrain veggie wraps and a low-calorie apple crumble. This sounds interesting.* As the next mail opened up, she gasped.

Bewildered, she looked at the date and time of the mail. It was written and sent on Sunday evening…*when she was alive.* It was sent from her iPhone, probably while she was waiting to board the flight back to Mumbai.

I'm soooo happy—Manav asked me to marry him! He's looking forward to building a life with my kids and me. I was apprehensive to leave my kids but when he suggested I bring them along, I was overjoyed! I cannot tell you what a validation this is. I was right all along; we are meant for each other. Things haven't been good between Neel and me for a long time but I stuck around because of the kids and because I wasn't sure if Manav felt as strongly. I'm going to get home and tell Neel everything! He has always had his doubts—time to put him out of his misery. I can finally start living my life on my terms now.

I just had to share with you—I'm counting on your support because it's not going to be easy hereon. But, I will survive. As long as I know how to love, I know I'll stay alive!

Lots of love,

Aisha

Siya couldn't believe it! Manav had agreed to marry Aisha? Wow! And, he wanted to embrace her kids too! Then why did Aisha overdose on sleeping pills? She was flummoxed. She immediately dialled Samar's number to share the contents of the email with him. As she read it out loud, her eyes settled on the names of the recipients. It was addressed to someone beside her—Arunima. *Oh God, so Arunima also knew about this!* "Samar, do you think Arunima had already read this when we met yesterday? But, she was consoling Neel so genuinely...how could it be?"

"I'm not sure. What should we do now that we know? This email subtly implicates him. What do you think, Siya?"

"Gosh, I can't believe it. I don't even know what to think. Do you think Neel could do this?" As they deliberated over it, Siya heard the insistent tone of another call on the line. As she took the phone off her ear to check the home screen for Caller ID, she froze. It was from Aisha's phone.

Mumbai, December 2004

I'll be there for you—The Rembrandts

I remember when I was pregnant for the first time after marriage. As a wave of nausea swept over me every now and then, I would recall those days when the smell of early morning cooking and a myriad other odours bothered me so much that I'd retch. Luckily, this time I knew what it was on account of.

When I went to see a doctor, my husband came along, beaming. How different everything was... When she asked if it was my first time, I hesitated. She waited. My eager beaver of a husband chimed in that it was! He saved me from blurting out what was uppermost in my mind. The guilt of my past deed was always hanging over my head. In my mind, I constantly replayed the sequence of events and wondered what else I could have (nay, should have) done. Every time I came up with the same answer. I could never have had it. It was just not possible.

The doctor was experienced and knowledgeable in the way she asked questions and prescribed tests and medicines. She told us when the baby would be due. I could actually look forward to the date!

To placate myself, I promised the one in my womb that I would try to do the right thing this time around. I would let no harm come to my baby. I would take care to nourish him/her as prescribed and try to be the best mother I could.

45

Two weeks later, Octavius

Deja vu. A room full of white clad people seated on the floor of Aisha's drawing room. The fragrance of incense enveloped the room as the faint strains of devotional music filled the air. The Ragi singers were setting up their musical instruments in front of a blow up of Aisha's smiling face.

"Looks like she will just step out of the photo to give me a hug," Siya whispered to Arunima. Arunima nodded in affirmation as she squeezed her arm affectionately.

The last few days had been so traumatic after Arunima had called Siya from Aisha's phone. They'd decided to confront Neel together with Aisha's email. Neel had broken down and confessed that he'd slipped in sleeping pills in Aisha's wine. He was livid when she'd told him she wanted to divorce him and marry Manav. What's more, she'd said she would take the kids too. He tried to placate her with reason and logic but she wouldn't budge. He couldn't bear to lose her and his kids. So, he chose to let her go.

'Crime of passion' is how the police termed it. Neel had been taken away to be tried in a court of law. Arunima and Siya were in shock for a couple of days. Arunima gathered herself up soon to look after Aisha's kids. She'd decided to take them with her to Delhi. She didn't want them to witness any more ugliness. The prayer meeting was organised for everyone to bid farewell and pray for Aisha's soul.

Siya stepped forward as Maya and Imran entered the hall. She motioned for them to sit beside her after they folded their hands and laid some rose petals at Aisha's photo. The Ragi addressed the gathering, stating the purpose for which they had gathered together. As he listed out the names of the family members present, soft sobs could be heard. Aisha's kids were huddled around their *maasi*, Arunima, as she held them close. Siya reached out to pat their heads even as her heart went out to them. *So small they are! What are they going to do without her?*

As the rich baritone of the Ragis launched into profound *shabads*, the eyes of those around her automatically closed. Looking around at the large number of people, Siya wondered how Aisha had connected with each person there. *Aisha came into my life again only to help me change it for the better. She must have agonised over the same things after she had her kids in a foreign country; that's why she empathised with me. She was not being calculative or diplomatic, she did it out of love. How many people do things selflessly, without expecting anything in return? Sadly, she never got her share of love. That's why she pursued Manav. Could she have made things work better with Neel? Who knows...no one knows what happens behind closed doors. She must have definitely tried. If she'd tried harder, she would have still been around. I know I'm being selfish. I would have loved to have her around. But then she would have lived an unhappy life. And, I wouldn't want that for her. I admire her for pursuing her dream but... So, what am I trying to achieve with Siddhant? I'm not unhappy. Then why am I pursuing him? What void can he possibly fill now?* Siya was nonplussed. *Oh my God, I didn't even think about it that way. I've been so consumed with losing weight and so proud of my achievements that I want to rub it in his face. Of course, I want him to regret what he did but how is it going to help now, after all these years? I am lucky that the choices I made worked out in my favour. How have the choices he made panned out? He leads a lonely life, devoid of companionship and love. Poetic justice, if you ask me.*

Looking up at Aisha's photo, she said—*thank you.*

As the kirtan concluded, everyone stood up. Arunima didn't want the kids to stand around absorbing any more despair. She signalled for Siya to take them into their room. Imran and Maya joined her. Maya's eyes teared up as the kids clung to Siya. "Siya, I think the kids would benefit from counselling. They have been through a lot. I would be happy to talk to them at a good time," Imran offered.

"That's so kind of you, Imran. I will speak with Arunima. She's their guardian from now."

Imran and Maya asked the kids to show them their favourite toys and books. Siya smiled as they engaged them in conversation, softly.

After returning home, Siya tried to take a nap, feeling exhausted with the constant whirring of her thoughts. She drifted in and out of sleep. When the kids returned from school, they ran to cuddle up beside her on the bed. With their small arms twisted around her, she felt the pain subsiding. She hugged them back fiercely, thankful for their unconditional love.

Later, she sat on the balcony with a cup of tea, watching the sun work its magic on the surface of the lake. As the sun lowered itself in the sky, the clouds came running towards it, begging it to stay longer, seducing it with their scarlet and violet hues. But, the sun's heart was elsewhere. It had been looking into the depths of the lake for so long that it was irresistibly drawn to its placidity. It wanted to douse itself in the cool waters of the lake, knowing that it was the only way the fire that had been burning inside it all day, could be put out. *Everything has a place and a function in Nature.*

It works mostly like clockwork. I wish it was the same with humans. I wish we were all programmed to perform a set of functions and our paths were clearly chalked out instead of being beset with dilemmas. The choices we have to make, the challenges that life poses us, she sighed.

Choices, that's what separates us from animals. We are given the power to make a choice that can alter the course of our life—that is a powerful tool. In the end, we are a sum of all the choices we have made. We must choose wisely. But the catch is, wisdom only comes after making mistakes. We can't even imagine the ramifications of our choices when we make them. Gosh, what a gamble it is! If it works out well then it was a choice well made; if not, then…

"Didi, I'll be taking the kids down to the park. Do you want anything?" Vaishali asked softly, trying to not intrude for long.

"Another cup of tea would be great, Vaishali." Siya answered.

"Make that two," said Samar, joining her on the balcony.

"How come you are home so early? I didn't even hear the doorbell ring," Siya asked.

"The boys opened the door. I wanted to be with my wife so I told my boss I had to go," he smiled. Siya smiled back at him, thanking the stars for the little voice that had pushed her to make the right choice.

46

The next morning, as Siya walked to the gym, she reflected on the events of the last couple of days. Aisha had left a deep void. Regret would be woven into the fabric of Siya's life going forward. But, she had also bequeathed her many happy memories. *It's best to remember her with affection rather than regret.*

I must call Arunima to check when she is heading back to Delhi. And, also what's happening to Neel? Wonder how the kids are coping... I need to send an email to Siddhant about our meeting. I must call Manoj to find out if he has any writing assignments for me. I need to distract myself, this thinking all the time will make my head explode! I should ask Maya how her meeting with the artists went. It would be nice to get involved in the Art retreat. Knowing Maya, she will plan it beautifully!

As she walked into the gym, she could sense some activity. All the trainers and staff were walking around, talking to members. Siya was walking towards the locker room when a familiar voice called out, "Hi, Siya!" Turning around, Siya smiled as she saw Ira. Coming up to her, Ira explained that the gym was conducting a competition for all its members. It involved some basic workout routines along with a cardio test. Pulling her along to the gym floor, Ira beckoned a trainer to come over.

The trainer walked up to them with a form in hand. "Ma'am, you want to participate in this competition?" Siya smiled as Ira nodded animatedly on her behalf. "Ok. I need your name, age and weight before we begin." Walking her to a weighing machine after he made a note of her name and age, he asked her to remove her shoes and get on it. Siya did as she was told, looking straight ahead.

"Fifty-two kilos," he said out loud, before making a note.

"What?" Siya shrieked. "That's not possible, please check again. Ira, can you please have a look?" instructed Siya.

As Ira bent down to read the digital display, Siya's eyes bored into her head. Turning up to face her, she said, "It is fifty-two. Is that good or bad?" she asked, unsure.

"Yoohoo!" said Siya as she climbed off the machine. "I've lost it, I've lost it! I've finally lost the last two kilos!" she said, prancing around happily. Ira and the trainer watched her with a grin on their faces.

As Siya piped down, Ira walked over excitedly and said, "You've done it, woman. Take a good look at yourself," she said, making her face the full-length mirror. Dressed in leopard print tights and a sleeveless black top with her hair pulled back in a ponytail, Siya looked slim, happy and at peace. "Listen to the song that's playing," Ira said pointing upwards, to the in-house music system

I believe in miracles,
where you from,
you sexy thing, sexy thing you
I believe in miracles,
Since you came along
You sexy thing.

"Oh, I do! Life is made up of many such small miracles," she said, hugging Ira.

47

Four Seasons Hotel, Worli, 7:30 pm

Siya decided to check her hair and makeup in the lobby washroom before heading to the rooftop bar. The black dress really showed off her toned arms and shoulder blades. She'd applied some shimmering lotion on her exposed back and arms to amp up the glam quotient. She was nervous and excited but, she had to do this.

As she travelled up in the elevator, she kept checking her phone for messages. When the elevator doors opened on the rooftop, Siya was zapped. Walking into the Aer Skybar, Siya's gaze took in the stunning 360 degree view of the Mumbai skyline. *Great choice!* she thought. Her eyes roamed the crowd of Mumbai's elite, all dressed very fashionably, till they alighted on the face she was looking for.

Making her way to the table he was seated at, she marvelled at how dapper he looked in a suit. *Must make it a point to tell him.* He stood up to greet her as she got closer. "You look ravishing, Siya," he couldn't help saying.

"You look dapper too," Siya reciprocated, her heart beating just a little bit faster. Gulping a sip of water from the glass placed on the table, she tried to steady her nerves. Just then, the waiter showed up with a bottle of champagne for him to check.

"I've asked for a Moet & Chandon to celebrate this evening. I hope that's okay?" he asked, shyly. Siya's eyes widened even as she nodded at him.

The waiter proceeded to pop the champagne and poured it for them. "Enjoy your evening," he said, placing the bottle in an ice bucket next to their table and excusing himself.

As they clinked their glasses together and took a sip each, Siya felt tickled by the bubbles in her mouth as they slid smoothly down her throat. Bracing herself for the monologue she'd prepared, she said, "I should have done this a long time back. The reason we are here today..."

Siya's voice quivered with emotion as goosebumps gave her the chills on a pleasant August evening. He reached out to stroke her palm, with concern creasing his brow. She had to pause because the lump in her throat forced her to fight back the tears every now and then. His gaze never left her face. It was like he was travelling with her through the ups and downs of her life—the darkest moments too. He sensed her loneliness, her helplessness, even her anger and need for closure. His eyes welled up.

"I thought I had gotten over things and moved on. Little did I know that these feelings are buried inside me—this lethal concoction of guilt, rejection, unrequited love, and failure which I've been sipping at. To vindicate myself, I did what I had to do—write emails, share pictures of my new avatar, and even flirted lightly."

That brought a smile to his face. "I wish I was there with you then, Siya. I would have never left you alone." She looked up at him as his grip on her hand tightened. "In fact, I promise to never leave you alone...even if you're being pig-headed or I'm being a jerk."

Siya burst out laughing through the tears that were swimming in her eyes. Picking up the napkin lying on the table, she dabbed at her eyes, hoping no one was looking at her. "I wouldn't have chosen such a fancy place if I'd known I'd cry like this!" she muttered.

"I love you, sweetheart," he whispered.

"I love you more, Samar," she replied, as her gaze fell on his dimples.

"Shall we order something to eat?" he asked.

"Yes, please. I thought you'd never ask!" Siya teased, as a waiter appeared to refill their glasses.

Acknowledgements

This book is dedicated to a companion who has been with me through the highs and lows of life in many different avatars—Chai! The Beatles need love; all I need is one cup , three times a day!

Without a doubt, the credit for instilling this germ of writing a novel goes to my husband, Murali. He is the one who planted it and believed I could do it which is why I love him a little more with every passing day.

Thank you, Kanchana Banerjee, for kicking my ass to ensure I accomplished it. She used to bug me so much that I actually started avoiding her even though we are neighbours! You know I love you, darling.

Many thanks to Dipankar Mukherjee, for his patience and encouragement. I secretly believe that this book was meant to be birthed by him!

Thank you, Lakshmi, Preeti, Mallika, and Harini for your valuable inputs on my manuscript. Thanks to all my friends and family (Vikram, Rebecca, Mamta and Murali) who have read and loved this novel in parts and as a whole at different stages. I am so lucky to have you all as my cheerleaders.

Heartfelt thanks to this immense Universe that has given me so much and so generously.

Anuradha Ramachandran
Gurgaon, 2022

About the Author

An English Literature graduate from Delhi University, Anuradha gave up her corporate job to enjoy bringing up her kids. As they grew, she toyed with different ideas to keep herself gainfully occupied. Writing came back to her as a manna from the heavens! She rekindled her love for writing by doing freelance assignments with websites/publications in Mumbai.

After spending 14 years in a city that can easily get under your skin, she moved to Gurgaon. Amidst all the upheaval that followed, her writing helped her to connect with new people and explore her passions some more. She continued to write articles/stories to hone her writing skills which eventually culminated in her first novel, *The Secret of a Telltale Diet*.

A foodie at heart, she enjoys baking for friends and family!

Books, fitness, art, music, movies, aesthetics, wine, word games, travelling, nature—are some of her favourite things!

Readomania

Readomania exists to nurture, curate, and bring to you content you love. We are a publishing house that takes pride in encouraging talent, new or old, and provides a wonderful platform for awesome stories.

We make this possible in multiple ways.

The first as an independent publishing house. Readomania boasts of multiple imprints across various categories—fiction, nonfiction, children, to name a few. An eclectic mix of content for its readers, when you read a Readomania title, you enter a world that's yours, supported by unique and quality narratives.

The second, as an online publishing platform for writers—a place to share stories, poems, opinions, travelogues, a way to explore your creative talent. Available as premium, as well as free-to-read content across multiple genres, the reader is spoilt for choice.

Join us in this journey, as we explore, develop, and present stories to our readers and audiences. Welcome to the world of Readomania, get ready to craft stories that enrich lives.

You can visit us at: www.readomania.com